ROAD TO NIRVANA

ROAD TO NIRVANA

A Play in two acts

Arthur Kopit

A Dramabook

HILL and WANG

The Noonday Press

NEW YORK

Library of Congress Cataloging-in-Publication Data
Kopit, Arthur L.
Road to Nirvana : a play / Arthur Kopit.
p.   cm.
I. Title.
PS3561.O646R6   1991
812'.54—dc20
91-11144
CIP

To the Actors Theatre of Louisville,
whose generous commission enabled me to write
this play, and especially to
Jon Jory and Michael Dixon

Introduction

We have been publishing Arthur Kopit's plays for more than thirty years, starting with *Oh Dad, Poor Dad, Mamma's Hung You in the Closet and I'm Feelin' So Sad*. From the outset we knew that *Road to Nirvana*, perhaps because it is so strong, would offend some and perhaps be misunderstood by others. And this has proved true as the play moved from Louisville (where it was given its premiere at the Actors Theatre under its original title, *Bone-the-Fish*) to Houston, Cambridge, and most recently to New York. It was widely acclaimed as brilliant, powerful, and hilarious satire; some voices attacked it with unusual harshness and bitterness, calling it childish, banal, imitative, pornographic. Complaints from watchdogs of artistic mores have even reached the United States Senate, since Circle Repertory Theatre, which produced the play in New York, has received funding from the National Endowment of the Arts.

With this experience of diametrically opposed opinions in hand, it seemed to be more interesting to introduce the play not with one voice but with extended commentary from prominent playwrights, novelists, and a critic. We hope that their perceptions of the play will stimulate further discussion of Mr. Kopit's work. We are, of course, very much in their debt, and I should like to thank them for their contribution to this unusual introduction.

ARTHUR W. WANG

JOHN GUARE: In *Oh Dad, Poor Dad,* Arthur Kopit gave us the memorable Madame Rosepettle, a monstrous powerhouse controlling people's lives. *Indians* explored Buffalo Bill and the myths of our culture's first pop figures, while *Wings* dealt with the pathological tragedy of the loss of language. Now, after the underappreciated *End of the World with Symposium to Follow,* Kopit has gone happily round the bend and pounded all these together into a fun-house mirror called *Road to Nirvana.* The mirror reflects horrifically and hilariously a pop culture that must have had a stroke if these are the creatures and language of our collective dreams.

JOHN LAHR: *Road to Nirvana* ventures where few satires dare: into the dissonant world of the grotesque. How do you convey the burning rapacity of the Hollywood dream? the craven appetite to score at any price? The spiritual vacuum has to be made sensational; that is, the emptiness must be felt. And that is Arthur Kopit's considerable accomplishment. As Flannery O'Connor has written of the grotesque: "To the hard-of-hearing you shout, to the almost blind you draw large and startling pictures." *Road to Nirvana* is certainly a startling picture and, by my lights, as funny as it is well written.

ROBERT STONE: Few playwrights have explored so many aspects and dimensions of the human condition as Arthur Kopit. Always refusing the obvious, his work represents the highest kind of satire, one that recognizes the complexity of its targets, the complexity of things themselves.

Now, with his customary audacity and wit, Kopit has written

the outrageous, hilarious payoff to every Hollywood horror story. He makes a relentlessly logical examination of an infinitely illogical process, and the result is the most exhilarating sort of humor—unpredictable, merciless, and irresistible. While fulfilling all its comic intentions, *Road to Nirvana* constitutes a serious statement about the high-rolling movie mentality. It contains some of the funniest things ever written about the picture business, and also the truest.

ROBERT BRUSTEIN: *Road to Nirvana* may very well be one of the meanest plays ever written; it is certainly one of the funniest. Scorching the stage in angry reaction to David Mamet's *Speed-the-Plow*, *Road to Nirvana* (originally called *Bone-the-Fish*) is a satire on a satire, featuring the same breed of cynical and greedy manipulators operating in the same ravenous atmosphere of Hollywood sleaze. But whereas *Speed-the-Plow* featured Madonna as an actress in one of the central roles, Kopit casts her (under the thinly disguised name of Nirvana) as a character in the play, thereby exposing the equivocal moral posture of the Lincoln Center Broadway production. It is well known that Mamet's penetrating comedy about the deals Hollywood producers make, and the lies they tell, in order to maximize the profits of their films, was seriously compromised by the exploitation of the celebrated performer with no stage experience, to maximize the profits of the show. Inspired to ecstatic fury by these moral contradictions, Kopit responds by imagining a Hollywood populated by piranhas caught in a feeding frenzy, who would sacrifice their friends and family, their remaining values, even their own physical parts, to ensure a bankable film.

As the title suggests, Kopit has conceived *Road to Nirvana* as another "Road" picture, with Al and Jerry cast as Bing Crosby and Bob Hope. But, in place of the ingenue usually played by Dorothy Lamour, Kopit provides us with a drug-addled playmate named Lou, then the ditzy pop singer Nirvana, whose brains are so soaked in acid she has forgotten all the details of her life. To illustrate the epic scope of sex, greed, and power, Kopit also literalizes the various metaphors associated with the means to success—giving blood, eating shit, sacrificing a ball—thus demonstrating how venal and ambitious men give the kiss to hypocrisy behind the back of sentiment and idealism. *Road to Nirvana* is a ferocious scatological play, all the more funny for being true.

CARLOS FUENTES: It must have been an old Swiss who said that myths are lived unconsciously by most people but that a man or woman without a myth is a shelterless person. California is a place without roofs, but its people live the oldest myths of humanity in an unconscious and therefore particularly brutal manner. Arthur Kopit has made an extraordinary ritual out of the myth of Hollywood, its tribal mores, its transformation of the ageless potlatch of rival clans into something called the Deal, its demanding, sacrificial retribution for the excesses of success and failure. You expect a "Road" movie: *Road to Nirvana*, the twin sister of Utopia. You expect Hope and Crosby and Lamour: here they are, proving that all roads lead to the real Zanzibar, the real Morocco, the jungle and the desert in Beverly Hills, where the cyclorama and the painted sunsets and the sound stage have taken over nature, have become nature, so that it is the world outside the set that looks like a set. Here are Abbott and Costello eternally arguing, in a vicious verbal circle, about "Who's on first." But this time the quips are deadly, the insults are literal: every word in Kopit's play bears down on us, on those who pronounce it, on those who receive it, with the brutal implacability of the literal: here shit *is* shit, not a word, not an insult, but a literal invocation of its own material self. The stylized scenery of Hollywood—the poolside terrace, the screening room, the freeway, the pricey restaurant—is transformed by Kopit into its ancient, barbarian, genetic space, the sacred zone of ritual murder, the pyramid, the temple, the secret chamber, the slaughterhouse, the splintered column to which the objects of our veneration and hatred are tied at the hour of dawn or crepuscule, better to be sacrificed so that the world may go on. Like the Amazon who must tear off her breast to shoot arrows better, like the Eunuch who must tear off his genitals to assure the chastity of the Goddess, Kopit's characters must surrender their manhood or their femininity to the Hollywood Deity, the Deal. It is but a part—the *damned* part, as Georges Bataille called it—of the consumer society. Everything that is produced must be consumed, or the economy would come to a dreadful stop. From the Los Angeles poolside rises the moan of the barbarian, the nightmare of the Aztec night, the whistle of the Teutonic horde: You must be sacrificed for the life of the gods and the survival of the earth. Who are the gods? Where is this earth? Whose is it? Why do all roads to Nirvana lead through castration and excrement? Is it worth it? What is a human life worth? What is the price of the Deal? These are some of the disturbing questions Kopit raises in his splendidly troubling, mediate and immediate theatrical ritual.

Road to Nirvana was first produced on March 10, 1989, under
the title *Bone-the-Fish*, at the Actors Theatre of Louisville, where
it opened as part of the thirteenth Humana Festival of New
American Plays. Subsequently, the play opened on March 15,
1990, at the Alley Theatre in Houston. It was produced in Cambridge at the American Repertory Theatre on March 28, 1990,
and in Wellfleet, Massachusetts, at the Wellfleet Harbor Actors
Theatre on August 2, 1990. *Road to Nirvana* opened in New York
at the Circle Repertory Company on March 7, 1991.

ROAD TO NIRVANA

CHARACTERS

Al
Lou
Jerry
Ramón
Nirvana

ACT ONE: Al's place. Day.
ACT TWO: Nirvana's place. That night.

ACT ONE

Poolside patio, rear of AL's *modest L.A. bungalow. Sliding doors at rear open to house. Palms at periphery. Jungle-like underbrush.*

AL, *in shorts and polo shirt, mirrored sunglasses, sits on one of three canvas chairs at a round table with awning, a bottle of Perrier and a glass in front of him. There are three place settings. By his side is a liquor cart. On top: several bottles of Scotch, more Perrier, an ice bucket, and a phone. On bottom shelf, a large leather envelope.*

Nearby is a chaise. LOU *(short for Louise) is on the chaise in a bikini, bottom only. A straw hat hides her face from the sun.*

AL *is staring at* LOU, *puzzled.*

AL: If you don't want sun, what're you doin' in the sun?

LOU: I dunno.

Pause.

AL: I mean, to me, that's just fuckin' dumb.

LOU: It feels good. (AL *glances at his watch*) If you had tits you'd know what I meant.

AL: They're gonna burn t' fuckin' cinders!

LOU: I've got sunblock on.

AL: I don't understand the world anymore.

LOU: When did you?

AL: Once.

LOU: Bullshit.

AL (*Pointing at LOU*): *Bullshit!*

LOU: When?

AL: None of your business.

LOU: The last time you understood the world was when you were suckin' from your mother's tit. (*Beat*) That's why you want me to cover up. (*Beat*) I remind you of your mother.

AL: Lou, I am trying to stay off drugs and booze today. You are not helping.

Silence.

LOU: . . . So what time is it *now*?

AL: He'll be here!

LOU: Five hours late.

AL: He's an hour fuckin' late!

LOU: I don't think he's comin'.

AL: Jerry says he's comin', he is *comin'!*

LOU: Right.

AL: I'm tellin' ya!

LOU: We'll see.

AL: Hey!

LOU: I said we'll see.

AL: He'll be HERE!

LOU: Fine.

AL: Jerry gives his word on something, you can count on it!

LOU (*Flat*): Good.

AL: Fuck you!

LOU: I said good.

AL: And I am tellin' you, his word's like his fuckin' bond.

LOU: Then probably he'll be here.

AL: NO PROBABLYS! I know this guy! He says a thing, you can
fuckin' COUNT on it! You can bet your fuckin' life on it!
Jerry does not fuck you over!

LOU: . . . And you guys were *friends*?

AL: You are fuckin' somethin'.

LOU: Sure ain't *you*.

AL: What?

LOU: Nothin'.

VOICE (*From offstage*): Al . . . ?

AL: You see? You gotta believe in me more! (*Calling*) WE'RE
IN BACK! (*To Lou*) Now cover up.

LOU: I thought he was your friend.

AL: Lou—

VOICE: WHERE?

AL: AROUND THE SIDE, THEN BACK! (*To Lou, menacing*)
I don't want him getting any wrong ideas.

LOU (*Facetious*): Oh.

AL: Put it on!

*Lou reluctantly puts on her top. It does not provide much cov-
erage. Enter JERRY, from the side.*

JERRY: Al!

AL (*Rising*): Jerry!

JERRY: (*Re his watch, embarrassed*): I'm so—

AL: I knew you'd be here!

JERRY: The freeway—

AL: Hey!

JERRY (*Beside himself with apologies*): I was, like—

AL: You're HERE! (*They hug, slap each other's back, seem near tears*) Fuckit, man, fuckit!

JERRY: Jesus!

AL: Been too long.

JERRY: Too long!

AL: Too fuckin' long!

JERRY: Mustn't happen again.

AL: Never!

JERRY: Never again!

AL: Never fuckin' again!

JERRY: You said it!

AL: Why'd it happen?

JERRY: Who knows? It happened!

AL: Never fuckin' again.

JERRY punches AL. AL punches JERRY. They spar. They wrestle. LOU has removed her straw hat to watch.

JERRY (*Finally*): Look. I'm almost in tears.

AL (*Re his own eyes*): Wha'dya think these are?

JERRY: Fuckin' Jesus.

AL: Man! My God!

JERRY: Too good.

AL: Too fuckin' good.

JERRY: We gotta do this more.

AL: Like every fuckin' day.

JERRY: You got it.

AL (*Whispers, overcome with emotion*): *I love ya*, man.

JERRY (*Moved*): Oh shit.

AL: No, I mean it man, that's it, that's fuckin' it. I love ya. What more can I say?

JERRY: Same here.

AL: Is it?

JERRY: *Is* it?

AL: I mean, you're not just sayin' it?

JERRY: Sayin' it? Shit, man, I love ya!

AL: Despite everything?

JERRY: Hey!

AL: Right. That's in the past.

JERRY: What's past is past.

AL: You said it.

JERRY: I *believe* it, too.

AL: I do, too.

JERRY: Fuckin'-A.

AL: Shit!

JERRY: I'm in tears.

AL: We gotta do this more.

JERRY: Takes too much outta ya doin' it like, you know—

AL: Like this.

JERRY: Like this, right.

AL: Right.

JERRY: I mean—

AL: —like I'm already drained.

JERRY: Wiped out.

AL: Fuckin' wipeout, seein' you like this!

JERRY: Phew!

AL: Hey! You look fabulous.

JERRY (*Modest*): Nah!

AL: Really! Fuckin' fabulous! And I don't say things like that! I don't bullshit.

JERRY: Hey!

AL: All right, so I bullshit. Am I bullshitting now? No. You know it, too. You *know* you look fabulous! Lou, does he look fabulous?

LOU: Fabulous.

AL: You remember Lou.

JERRY: No.

AL: No?

LOU: We never met.

AL: Never met? Right! You never . . . Right. Jerry, this is Lou. Lou, this is Jerry. How come you guys never met?

JERRY: You kept her out of sight.

AL: *Right!* Why?

JERRY: Meryl.

LOU: Cunt.

AL: Hey! Come on! That's not nice. Meryl. Right. (*To* JERRY) But you *heard.*

JERRY: What?

AL: Of Lou, am I right? You must've heard me talk of her. I mean, when Meryl wasn't around.

JERRY: All the time.

AL: Tell Lou what you heard.

JERRY: It was very glowing.

AL: Now you see why. Lou, stand up, let Jerry see ya full. (*LOU stands*) Was I wrong?

JERRY: Fantastic!

AL (*To LOU*): You see? Everybody thinks you're fantastic. (*To JERRY*) She has no self-esteem. She thinks she's shit. Can you believe it? Woman looks like this, thinks she's shit. (*To LOU*) Would I be living with someone who was shit?

LOU: What about Meryl?

AL: Meryl was my wife. Wives turn *into* shit. That's why we're not getting married. I don't want you becoming what you think you are. (*To JERRY*) She's gonna go to a shrink.

JERRY: She should.

AL: I think so. (*To LOU*) Sit down.

LOU: I gotta go to the john.

AL: So go. You need to ask? Hey! (*Exit LOU. To JERRY sotto voce*) *I've just made her my partner.*

JERRY: Hey!

AL: Lou's got like enormous untapped talent.

JERRY: That's just great.

AL: Been a real big ego boost.

JERRY: I'm sure.

AL: Not that you'd notice it.

JERRY: Partner in what?

AL: In what? In business.

JERRY: Which is . . . ?

AL: Are you kidding me?

JERRY: I don't read the trades anymore.

AL: What's the one thing I know how to do? (*JERRY stares at him*) . . . Tell me you're putting me on. (*JERRY laughs*) My heart almost stopped.

JERRY: So, you're back in films.

AL: Back?

JERRY: Last I heard, you'd been fired.

AL: Four years ago!

JERRY: I'm in a different world.

AL: Jerry, never count on a studio for loyalty. You got out in time.

JERRY: Well—

AL: No! I mean, least you knew who did you in. Right or wrong is not the point. A person did you in! Flesh and blood. When

my time came, it was like some, you know, mountain.
"Thanks. Goodbye." It was fuckin' Xeroxed! "Dear Producer." Not so much as my fuckin' name. I thought maybe
it's not me. It's me. I said, No way am I goin' back with a
fuckin' studio.

JERRY: Did they ask?

AL: Who?

JERRY: The studios.

AL: Ask *me*?

JERRY: Yeah.

AL: With *my experience*?

JERRY: 'Cause no studio asked me.

AL: Well, you're a different case.

JERRY: Why?

AL: You ask why?

JERRY: Yeah.

AL: I dunno.

JERRY: I mean, I worked with you.

AL: Right.

JERRY: They asked you.

AL: Right.

JERRY: Why not me?

AL: I dunno.

JERRY: I was frankly quite surprised.

AL: I'm surprised no one asked.

JERRY: That's why I'm surprised they asked you.

AL: Well, I *was*, you know, like, above you.

JERRY: Not by much.

AL: Jer, I think I've given you the wrong impression here. I was asked by just a *few* . . . major studios. Not all. Just a few.

JERRY: I'd have been glad for one.

AL: The point is, I'd made up my mind. I said, No way am I going back with something that's not flesh and blood. Lou helped me come to that. Helped me find the strength to say fuck you! Lou gave me that Fuck-You Strength. Did I ever say fuck you before? The truth.

JERRY: Every two minutes.

AL: I never meant it.

JERRY: No!

AL: Now I do. Jer, you've gotta be able to say fuck you! and mean it or you're fucked, and that's the fuckin' truth. And Lou has brought me to that truth. It's like—no bullshit!— something almost I'd say *spiritual*. It's like suddenly you've got this weird inner *light*! Enlightenment, Lou says, is what it is. I mean, you just like fuckin' *know* what like maybe,

say, Buddha felt. Or Moses. Gandhi. "FUCK YOU!" And
you mean it! Unbelievable. The Power. And the Truth.
Takes a lifetime of suffering to get to this!

JERRY: So who're you working for?

AL: No one.

Beat.

JERRY: . . . You're out of work?

AL: I've gone *independent*.

JERRY: Al!

AL: Inde-fuckin'-pendent!

JERRY: Al!

AL: Now *I* call the shots.

JERRY: That's great!

AL: And I'm *doin'* great. I've got like certain deals. I mean,
finally. Fuckin' scary bein' on your own. Very dark times I
have been through. I'm opening up to you now.

JERRY: I didn't know.

AL: How could you? Now you do. And Lou is who brought me
through. That is why I have made her my partner.

JERRY: Good for you!

AL: The woman saved my life!

JERRY: You've done the right thing.

AL: I *know* I have. I am a whole new man, thanks to her. Tell me. Say no if you can't. Can you notice it?

JERRY stares at AL.

JERRY: . . . Not sure.

AL: Some can, some can't.

JERRY: Wait. I think I can.

AL: Where?

JERRY: Hard to say.

AL: Like . . .

JERRY: All over.

AL: Right. That's it. It's all over me. I'm completely new. Jer, what I was with that cunt Meryl was another man. What happened between you and me was the workings of a demon. What I was back then was fuckin' *evil*.

JERRY: Forget it.

AL: I can't. It preys on my mind. You should've come and fuckin' killed me for what I did to you.

JERRY: It wasn't worth it.

AL (*Suddenly cold*): What's that supposed to mean?

JERRY: Means I didn't think you were worth killing.

AL: Well, what kinda fuckin' thing is that to say?

JERRY: I dunno.

AL: I thought this was all past.

JERRY: It is.

AL: Well then, what—

JERRY: I mean—

AL: Suddenly!

JERRY: You asked.

AL: I asked? I asked what?

JERRY: Why I didn't kill you.

AL: Bull*shit*! I said I can't figure OUT why you didn't kill me. SAID! Didn't ask. Said.

JERRY: Sorry.

AL: I didn't mean to open up a whole fuckin' discussion.

JERRY: Man—

AL: No offense.

JERRY: I just—

AL: Forget it! No offense.

JERRY: I must've misunderstood.

AL: How can you say I wasn't worth killing?

JERRY: Al—

AL: No. Forget it, man.

JERRY: Al, look—

AL: Hey! Forget it.

JERRY: Al—

AL: I just can't believe—

JERRY: I *considered* killing you, all right?

AL (*Guardedly hopeful*): . . . You did?

JERRY: Yes!

AL: You're not just saying that?

JERRY: No! Really, man. I gave it very serious consideration.

AL: Jer, thank you. That's all I wanted to hear. The reasons you didn't, keep 'em to yourself.

JERRY: What's past is past.

AL: What's past is past!

JERRY: Could I have a drink?

AL: Hey! Sure. Sorry, man. What kind of host am I? Scotch, right?

JERRY: Right.

AL: On the rocks.

JERRY: Neat is fine.

AL: Neat it is. (*He pours*)

JERRY: When'd you get this place?

AL: 'Bout two years ago.

JERRY: It's nice.

AL: It's a step. (*He hands JERRY the drink. JERRY drinks it down. AL studies JERRY as he drinks. JERRY finishes*) Another?

JERRY: Better put a splash of water in.

AL does as asked, eyes on JERRY.

AL: And you?

JERRY: What?

AL: Doin' well?

JERRY: Okay.

Pause.

AL: You're sure *lookin'* great. (*He hands JERRY the new drink*)

JERRY: I run a lot. (*He drinks. AL watches him*)

AL: Well, it shows.

JERRY: Sometimes I swim.

AL: Before you came I was like, you know, afraid—

JERRY: I'm fine.

AL: I can see. (*Pause*) And Susan?

JERRY: Who?

AL: I mean Sarah—what's wrong with me?

JERRY: She died.

AL: *Died?*

JERRY: Last year. You didn't know?

AL: *Know!?*

JERRY: Bad time.

AL: Jesus.

JERRY: Very, very bad.

AL: Wow . . .

JERRY: Real big loss. Very, very bad.

AL: I'm sorry, man!

JERRY: Thanks.

AL: If I'd known—

JERRY: Hey!

AL: Was it sudden?

JERRY: Very.

AL: Shit.

JERRY: Big, big loss.

AL: I wish you'd called.

JERRY: Why?

AL: I dunno. Might've helped.

JERRY: Who?

AL: Who? Helped you! What a fuckin' downer.

JERRY: What's past is past.

AL: Right. What's past is past. Damn straight! We go on. We survive. We are fuckin' tough! Here, take the bottle.

JERRY: No. Keep it there.

AL: Hey!

JERRY: Really. Keep it there.

AL: You still do coke?

JERRY: A bit. Not much.

AL (*Calls*): Lou! Bring some coke.

JERRY: No, I'm fine.

AL: We've got tons.

JERRY: I'm fine. Really. Scotch is fine. Seeing you again, I'm fine.

AL (*Punching JERRY*): Fuckit, man!

JERRY: I've been through a lot.

AL: I can see. (*Lifting his Perrier*) To better times.

JERRY (*Lifting his Scotch*): To better times.

LOU comes back.

AL: Susan died.

LOU: Who?

AL: I mean Sarah—shit, what's wrong with me.

LOU: Sarah who?

AL: Sarah Jerry.

LOU: That's too bad.

JERRY: Yeah.

AL: How about some 'ludes?

JERRY: No. Really. Scotch is fine.

AL: Just say the word.

JERRY: I will. Thanks.

LOU: Meth?

JERRY: Scotch is fine.

AL: Green giants, hash—

JERRY: If I want, I'll ask.

AL: You sure?

JERRY: I'm sure.

AL: So what's this place like where you're workin'? (*To Lou*) Jerry makes educational films.

LOU: Hey! For where?

JERRY: High schools, colleges.

AL: Like what?

JERRY: . . . What?

LOU: What are they about?

JERRY: How to get off drugs.

AL: Great.

JERRY: Booze.

AL: That's important stuff.

JERRY: We're doing one on AIDS right now.

AL: For high schools?

JERRY (*Nodding*): Colleges.

AL: Very crucial work. I like what I'm hearing here.

LOU: You gonna show condoms in the film?

JERRY: Yeah.

AL: Good. That's important. How?

JERRY: . . . How?

AL: I mean, do you show kids how to put them on, or what?

JERRY: We use diagrams.

AL: Fuck diagrams.

JERRY: Al, the Southern market won't—

AL: Fuck the Southern market. Make a Northern version and a Southern one.

JERRY: Even California won't—

AL: Hey, I'm telling you—free advice!—you make a version for cassette, you show someone like, say, Lou putting a rubber on the dick of a sixteen-year-old kid, it'll sell. I mean *sell*! Am I right?

JERRY: Look—

AL: AM I RIGHT?

JERRY: That's not the point.

AL: Not the *point*? We're talking education, man! I've got a daughter, twelve, almost in her teens; I ask her if she knows how to put a condom on a guy and she says no. You call that safe? I mean, is that the kind of world you want your fucking kids growing up in?

LOU (*Calming him*): Al.

AL: I get very exorcised on this point. Jerry, girls hafta learn how to put condoms on their guys. We are in a state of crisis in this land! And guys like you can show them how.

JERRY: I'll bring it up.

AL: Fuck it man, where's the spark? I don't see the spark! I'm looking for the spark; you walk in here, first thing I do, I look deep down into your eyes. Where's the spark? I don't see the spark.

JERRY: You do what you can.

AL: Fuck that.

LOU: Al—

AL: I'm talking to my friend! This is the dearest friend I ever had; I did him dirt once upon a time and I won't again. Get out o' that shit, I'm telling you.

JERRY: I'm doing what I can.

AL: You can do *more*.

JERRY: I'm not sure.

AL: I'm tellin' you.

JERRY: It's political.

AL: What?

JERRY: Educational films. They're political.

AL: Political?

JERRY: You need grants. School boards have the final say . . .

AL: How much do you make?

JERRY: Al—

AL: Come on.

JERRY: It's not—

AL: It *is*, I'm MAKIN' it my business. How much do you make?

JERRY: Al—

AL: Two hundred grand?

JERRY: Why'd you ask me here?

AL: To make amends.

JERRY: This is not the way.

AL: How much do you make?

JERRY: Al—

AL: Two hundred grand?

JERRY: Not even close.

AL: Three?

JERRY: The other way.

AL: *Less?*

JERRY: Yeah.

AL: Not less than a hundred?

JERRY: Yeah.

AL: Come on!

JERRY: I'm tellin' you.

AL: You're suckin' ass for less than a hundred grand?

JERRY: Al—

AL: I don't fuckin' believe my ears.

JERRY: It's not the money—

AL: Hey, don't bullshit me! You're suckin' dick and ass for less than a hundred grand! What the hell has happened to you, man?

JERRY: I have a percentage of the profits.

AL: On a film that shows how to put a rubber on by *diagram?*

JERRY: There are other films.

AL: Like on drugs.

JERRY: Yeah.

AL: Do they show how to like shoot up, snort, cook the stuff?

JERRY: No.

AL: Shit, man, profits; suck my dick, I'll give you profits. You are in a den of thieves. You are being had, man. I can't bear what I am seeing here. I could weep for what's become of you. How the fuck do you eat?

JERRY: I eat.

AL: Yeah, cold cereal. JOSÉ!

LOU: José is off.

AL: Who's the other one?

LOU: Ramón.

AL: RAMÓN!

Ramón appears at the door.

RAMÓN: ¿Si?

AL: What's the soup of the day?

RAMÓN: ¿Que?

AL: The *soup du jour*, the soup *de las días*, the SOUP OF THE DAY, DICKHEAD!

RAMÓN: Chicken soup.

AL: Bring my friend a bowl of chicken soup. (*Exit RAMÓN*) Man, if I had known—

JERRY: I like what I'm doing.

AL: So do I!

JERRY: I'm sure.

AL: But I'm at least being paid.

JERRY: I'm being paid.

AL: Like hell you're being paid. You're being HAD! I'm sorry, man, but I can't bear seeing you in misery.

JERRY: I'm not in misery.

AL: Jerry, you're in misery. (*To Lou*) Is he in misery?

LOU: Misery.

AL: Lou knows things, man. She's got like a sense. Misery is contagious! If I didn't love you so much I'd kick you the fuck out. (*JERRY starts to pour himself another drink*) Lou, help him with his drink. (*She does*) Jerry, you are dwelling in a very dangerous land, the Land of Misery. I know it well, for I have dwelt there myself. Jerry, beware. The Land of Misery knows no . . . FUCK!

JERRY: Compassion?

AL: No.

LOU: Bounds?

AL: No. Knows no . . .

JERRY: Tell me what you're trying to say.

AL: Get out. That is what I'm trying to say.

JERRY: To where?

AL: Here! To *me*! Come back and work with me. That's the truth, man; that is what I asked you here to say. I've missed having you around. No bullshit, man. (*AL is fighting tears. JERRY is astonished*) What's past is past. I want you back. (*RAMÓN enters with a bowl of soup*) Bring him another.

JERRY: This is fine.

AL: Hey! You don't want it, leave it. (*RAMÓN*) Another bowl of soup. (*RAMÓN stares back blankly*) Un otras bolas de soupas! (*RAMÓN leaves the bowl he's just brought and exits, puzzled*) The truth—when I asked you here for lunch, wha'dya think I was thinking of? (*JERRY shrugs*) You weren't thinking, Maybe Al's gonna ask me back? (*JERRY shakes his head*) I don't believe it.

JERRY: I didn't know *you* were back!

AL: But once you knew? (*JERRY shrugs*) Come on! You *had* to be hoping! (*JERRY shrugs*) You don't *miss* all this?

JERRY: Of course I do.

AL: And you weren't hoping that I'd ask you back? (*JERRY shrugs*) Hey!

JERRY: Sure, I was hoping that.

AL: Of course you were.

JERRY: How could I not?

AL: How could you *not*.

JERRY: It's not the money.

AL: I know that!

JERRY: I mean, like—

AL: The money's nice.

JERRY: But that's not it.

AL: Not even close!

JERRY: So. What is it?

AL: You tell me.

JERRY: Something maybe in our blood?

AL: In our BLOOD! YES! (*Pointing at Lou*) Lou?

LOU: What?

AL: What is it?

LOU: What is *what*?

AL: What's in our blood?

LOU: Our *blood*?

AL: That makes us, you know . . .

LOU: I dunno.

AL: It's the LIFE! Cursing through! The spark of fuckin' life! We're like fuckin' addicts! Addicts of life! (*To JERRY*) But the spark of life is not in your blood, Jer. No more! Am I right? Can't hear.

JERRY (*Barely audible*): Right.

AL: Of course I'm right. The spark is gone from you. Your eyes should have coins on their lids. *Life!* That's what's missing from your life! And you want it back again. Right? Am I right? Speak up. Can't hear!

JERRY (*Looking down*): Yeah.

AL: You wanna cry, go ahead, don't be ashamed. (*To Lou*) Do I cry?

LOU: All the time.

AL: Go ahead and cry.

JERRY: You really want me back?

AL: I want you back more 'n anything. You want me to crawl to you? I'll crawl. I love you, man. And I always have. (*JERRY starts to cry*) Good. Get it out. Let it out.

JERRY: I'm crying in the soup!

AL: There's another one coming, I look ahead, I know what's what, fuck the soup! (*AL knocks the bowl to the floor*) Jerry and Al, Al and Jerry. That's how it was. And how it's gonna be. I can't live without you, man.

JERRY (*Softly*): I thought you hated me.

AL: *Hated* you?

JERRY: In fact . . . (*He stares at AL, then turns away*)

AL: . . . What?

JERRY: Nothing.

AL: No, come on.

JERRY: It's *nothing!*

AL: Hey!

Beat. JERRY turns back and faces AL.

JERRY: I thought maybe you'd asked me here to do me in.

AL: Do you *in?*

JERRY: My mind's not exactly in the best of shape.

AL: Wow!

JERRY: Sorry.

AL: Do you *in?*

JERRY: It's me, not you.

AL: Jesus! (*RAMÓN arrives with the second bowl of soup. He looks down at the first in surprise and disgust. To RAMÓN.*) Just leave it and get out.

RAMÓN puts the second bowl near JERRY and leaves.

JERRY: I think finding Sarah, you know, in the bath . . .

AL: Jer—

JERRY: It was like . . .

AL: Jerry, lemme tell you something.

JERRY: Still think someday maybe I will wake and . . .

AL: Lemme tell you something, Jerry. Set your mind at ease.

JERRY: It's not at ease.

AL: No, it's not, I can tell. And I'd like it to be at ease.

JERRY: It's getting more at ease.

AL: Good. Lou, pour Jerry another drink. (*She pours*) Jerry. What I am about to confide is the God's honest truth. Jerry, I don't just love you, man. I love you so goddamn much I wish I was queer so I could fuck you, that's how much I love you, that's the fuckin' truth.

JERRY (*Moved*): . . . Al!

AL (*To Lou*): What'd I say to you last night?

LOU: You wished you were queer.

AL: Why?

LOU: So you could fuck Jerry.

AL: There you are, man. That's the fuckin' truth.

JERRY: Shit, I'm crying in the second bowl.

AL (*To Lou*): You see why I love this guy?

LOU: I gotta go to the john.

AL: Again?

LOU: I'm SORRY!

AL: Jesus Christ. (*She whispers something. He sighs, nods, waves her off. She leaves. To JERRY*) She's got something wrong with her bladder. She's like all fucked up inside. I think it's in her head. Man, I can't tell you how moved I am to see you here, like this, to talk with you, be with you. It's like you're me. I've been incomplete without you here. You know what I told Lou before you came? (*JERRY, sniffling, shakes his head*) I said, Jerry is a man you can count on. You know how often she's heard me say that about somebody I know? *Never!* You are like unique! I need you back. And I know you're gonna say yes. 'Cause I know you've missed this life.

JERRY: Wouldn't you?

AL: Frankly, I can't *contemplate* life without this life.

JERRY: Life without this life is not life.

AL: It's not. It's a fuckin' *holding* pattern!

JERRY: Wow.

AL: Jerry, this will fuckin' knock you out. This is like real weird shit. Lou went apeshit when I told her this. Two weeks ago, I am flying into L.A. from I think Nashville, maybe London—anyway, we can't land—smog, fog, shit, can't see anything, can't even see the wings. So we circle. And we circle. And I'm lookin' out. Hours pass. Nothin'! And I think, Jesus! this is what it must be like for Jerry, not being in the film business anymore!

JERRY: That's it.

AL: I got it right?

JERRY: That's fuckin' it.

AL: Even with like all those awards you've won?

JERRY: Like circling over no place.

AL: Unbelievable!

JERRY: The gods were angry with me, Al.

AL: That's what you thought?

JERRY: What have I done wrong, I thought.

AL: You thought *that*?

JERRY: Every day since I left!

AL: And I'm the one who did you wrong.

JERRY: Not true.

AL: It's true.

JERRY: No, Al, no; you made a judgment call.

AL: I fucked you over, man.

JERRY: It was a judgment call!

AL: I let business take precedence over heart.

JERRY: And you were right.

AL: Come on.

JERRY: You did the right fuckin' thing.

AL: You're saying that.

JERRY: No, I mean it, man. I could've torn your fuckin' head off!

AL: Right!

JERRY: Pulled your stupid fuckin' heart out bare-handed—

AL (*Overlapping JERRY*): Right! Right, man!

JERRY: Thrown your fuckin' guts to some decrepit dogs—

AL: And would I have blamed you? No.

JERRY: You made the right fuckin' call.

AL: You are a fuckin' prince.

JERRY: If the roles had been reversed—

AL: You'd have done the same.

JERRY: Fucked you over just as fast.

AL: You are a prince.

JERRY: And you are a king.

AL: So. Let's share the fuckin' kingdom.

JERRY: I'm with you.

AL: I mean it, man.

JERRY: So do I.

AL: No. I really mean it. Jer, I've got the kingdom *here*. (*He reaches to the serving cart and lifts the leather envelope*)

And I'm gonna share it with you. (*He puts it on the table.* JERRY *stares at it.* LOU *returns*) Feeling better?

LOU: Yeah.

AL: I am about to let Jerry see paradise.

LOU: Ahhhh.

JERRY: Paradise is inside this?

AL (*To LOU*): Pour Jerry another drink.

JERRY: I mean, what is this thing?

AL: An envelope.

JERRY: Come on!

AL: I think Jerry's getting excited.

LOU (*Pouring*): Don't blame him.

JERRY: What's *inside*?

AL: Jerry, what's inside is probably, conservatively speaking, the deal to end all deals.

JERRY: . . . And you're gonna share this with *me*?

AL: Have to have you in or it's no deal.

JERRY: What kind of deal is that?

AL: A deal with *contingencies.*

JERRY: Such as?

AL: There's a certain *quid pro quo* built in.

JERRY waits for more. No more comes.

JERRY: . . . This is not clear.

AL: The party we've been dealing with wants *assurances.*

JERRY: Of what?

AL: That we can deliver.

JERRY: What?

AL: The deal.

JERRY: I see. (*Pause*) . . . And that is *what?*

AL: What I've promised to deliver.

JERRY: Which is like what?

AL: A *film.*

JERRY: This is a *film* deal!

AL: I'm in the film *business!*

JERRY: It's beginning to make sense.

AL (*To Lou*): Maybe he shouldn't drink any more.

JERRY: Actually, I think it's helping.

AL: If you say.

JERRY: So why do you need me?

AL: Picture a pie.

JERRY: Right.

AL: This film is like that pie.

JERRY: Right.

AL: That pie is too big for Lou and me to eat alone. If we two tried to eat this pie alone we'd get sick.

JERRY: You're shitting me.

AL (*To Lou*): Am I shitting him?

LOU: I'm confused.

AL: About what?

LOU: The pie.

AL: The *pie*?

LOU: I don't understand the pie.

AL: The pie is symbolic of the film.

LOU: How?

AL: How? Big pie? Big film!

LOU: How do you eat a film?

AL: You don't eat a film!

LOU: Then I don't think it's a good symbol.

AL (*To Jerry*): Do you understand what I'm talking about?

JERRY: I'm not sure.

AL: FORGET THE FUCKING PIE! It's a *FILM*! Okay? *WE* can become the producers of this film if, and *only* if, we are able to convince the owner of said property that we can in fact produce!

JERRY: Right.

AL (*Re himself and Lou*): We can't handle it ourselves.

JERRY: Because the pie's too big.

AL: There you go!

JERRY (*Flat tone—still confused*): I'm excited.

AL: Good.

JERRY: Now could I please see what's inside?

AL: First I have to know you care.

JERRY: Would I be here if I didn't care?

AL: Care a *lot*!

JERRY: Al—

AL: I can easily get someone else.

JERRY: LEMME SEE THE FUCKIN' THING!

AL: Good. Now I know you care. (*To Lou*) Did you see the spark? (*To Jerry*) Jer, the spark is back!

JERRY: Al—

AL: Open.

JERRY opens the leather envelope and takes out a manuscript.
He stares at it.

JERRY: It's got no title.

AL: Right. Someone could see.

JERRY: It's that hot?

AL: Feel the cover.

JERRY (*Feeling the cover*): . . . Weird.

AL: Asbestos.

JERRY: No!

AL: The asbestos is symbolic. The code name for this project is
     Asbestos. When I say to you "Asbestos" . . .

JERRY: This is what you mean.

AL: Right.

JERRY: Al, how'd you get this thing?

AL: Don't ask.

JERRY: Why?

AL: Because you do not want to know.

JERRY: I do.

AL: You *think* you do.

JERRY: I don't?

AL: You don't.

JERRY: I thought I did.

AL: Take my word. It's for your own sake, Jer.

JERRY: Al—

AL: 'Nuf said. Open.

JERRY opens the cover and looks inside.

JERRY (*Reads*): . . . *Moby Dick?*

AL: And this is but the tip of the iceberg!

JERRY: Al, *Moby Dick* has been done.

AL: Says who?

JERRY: I saw the film!

AL: That's a different *Moby Dick.*

LOU: What's a Moby Dick?

AL: Biggest dick you ever saw.

JERRY: I will not be involved in a porno film!

AL: Did I say anything about a porno film? This is class!

JERRY: Al, there is only one *Moby Dick*. And it was written by Herman Melville.

LOU: This one wasn't.

JERRY: Great. Who wrote this?

AL: Don't ask.

JERRY: Al—

AL: I say that for your own benefit.

JERRY: Look—

AL: Would I put asbestos on just any cover?

JERRY: Al—

AL: *Moby Dick* is the title being used for the *moment*. Capische?

JERRY: Why?

AL: Because the author likes the sound.

JERRY: Who's the author?

AL: Turn.

JERRY turns the page.

JERRY: "An original screenplay by Charlene Samuels"? Who's Charlene Samuels?

AL: Not the author.

JERRY: So what's her name doing there?

AL: Protection.

JERRY: From . . . ?

AL: People discovering the author's name.

JERRY: Al—

AL: Our lives would be worth shit if people knew what we have.

JERRY: Including mine?

AL: Yours especially.

JERRY: Al, how am I to help with this if I don't know what I'm
helping with?

AL: In due time, you'll know.

JERRY: Due time being what?

AL: However long it takes us to decide if you can be trusted.

JERRY: You're not sure I can be *trusted*?

AL: Jerry! You said you wanted to *kill* me!

JERRY: I've gotten over that.

AL: Cut your wrist.

JERRY: What?

AL: Show me that you care.

JERRY: *What!?*

AL: I want to see some blood. Cut your wrist. Here. (*He hands JERRY a knife*)

JERRY: This is a butter knife, Al.

AL: RAMÓN!

JERRY: This is unbelievable.

Enter RAMÓN.

RAMÓN: ¿Si?

AL: Bring us a sharp knife.

Exit RAMÓN.

JERRY: Al—

AL (*To LOU*): Show him your wrists. (*She holds out her wrists. JERRY looks. Apparently he sees scars. AL holds out his wrists, too. The same. JERRY stunned*) The shedding of blood is a cleansing, bonding ritual. Lou and I have both shed blood for this. When we know you are with us to that same degree, you'll be let in on more. (*RAMÓN enters with a large, sharp knife*) Thank you, Ramón. (*RAMÓN leaves the knife and exits*) Okay, cut.

JERRY: Al—

AL: We're not asking you to *kill* yourself!

JERRY (*First hopeful thing he's heard*): . . . You're not?

AL: You know how many people in this town would cut their wrists for this?

JERRY: Al . . .

AL: It's *symbolic*!

JERRY: Look—

AL: Of loyalty!

JERRY: I know what it's symbolic of!

AL: If you don't cut, you're out.

JERRY: It'll HURT!

AL: Of course it'll hurt! That's the fucking point!

JERRY: Al—

AL: We need to know you care.

JERRY: Look.

LOU: I don't think he cares.

AL: He cares! I know this man! I've seen the spark! (*To JERRY*) Jerry, please. One little cut. We need to know you can be counted on.

JERRY: Al, I gotta tell you, this is scaring the shit out of me.

AL: One little cut!

JERRY: What about up here?

AL: No!

JERRY: Al—

AL: Across the wrists. One small cut!

JERRY (*Re the manuscript*): This thing better be worth it!

AL: You have my permission to cut my throat if it's not. (*JERRY perfunctorily moves the blade across a wrist. He stares down. So do AL and LOU. No blood comes*) You call that a cut?

JERRY: It felt like a cut.

AL: You couldn't cut through butter with that cut!

JERRY: Al—

AL: Cut your fuckin' wrists or you're out!

JERRY tries again. He holds his wrist up for AL and LOU to see. They peer closely.

JERRY: There!

AL: Where?

JERRY: Right there.

AL: So where's the blood?

JERRY: It's gonna come.

AL: The kind of cut I mean, blood comes!

JERRY: I felt a cut!

AL: Then how come there's no blood?

JERRY: You've gotta give these things a chance!

LOU picks up the knife.

LOU: Here, lemme try!

JERRY: No! (*He takes the knife from her*) I'll try again. (*But he can't*) Al, I can't.

AL (*To LOU*): I overestimated him.

JERRY: Al, I'm really freaked by this.

AL: I have hold of the hottest fucking property since the invention of film itself and you are playing pussy shit!

JERRY slices a wrist. He holds it up. Blood appears.

JERRY: Satisfied?

AL: Now the other one.

JERRY: Come on!

AL: The other wrist or you're out!

JERRY: I think I'm gonna faint.

LOU: Get rid of 'm.

JERRY: No! (*He takes the knife*) Then I'll have cut one wrist for nothing. I've cut one, I can cut 'em both!

AL: The first one's always the hardest.

JERRY: There!

They look.

LOU: Where? (*JERRY tries again. Again, nothing. To AL*) And
     this is the guy you thought we could count on!

*JERRY cuts again. Screams a bit. A drop of red appears. JERRY
looks as if he's about to faint. AL gets up, goes over and hugs
JERRY proudly. JERRY struggles to catch his breath.*

JERRY: Now . . . What's this all about?

AL: I am going to write a name on a piece of paper. You will
    read the name, say nothing, then eat the piece of paper. (*He
    starts writing on a napkin*)

JERRY: I don't think I heard you right.

AL: You heard right. No precaution is too great. (*AL slides the
    napkin over. JERRY looks down. The name startles him*) I
    take it you recognize the name.

JERRY: Nirva—

AL stops him with a gesture.

AL: What we have here is *her* life story.

JERRY: . . . *Moby Dick?*

AL: Eat the napkin.

JERRY: Al—

AL: Eat the fucking napkin.

JERRY: How about I just burn the thing?

AL: I want to see some COMMITMENT here!

JERRY (*Showing* AL *his wrists*): Al—

AL: What do you think a film of this woman's life would gross, domestic, in a week? I'm talking *authorized*.

JERRY: Al, this is *Moby Dick*.

AL: There's more to come.

JERRY: Great.

LOU: And she's giving us the rights to *all* of it!

JERRY (*Flat*): Well, that's just fabulous.

AL: *Option* on the rights.

LOU: Option.

AL: Right.

JERRY: It's *Moby*-fuckin'-*Dick*!

AL: Not entirely. (*Lowered voice*) She's changed Ahab's name to hers, and made the whale a cock.

JERRY: Al—

AL: So she's nuts! Does that make her life less valuable?

AL stares at JERRY. *JERRY stares back. He begins to think. Long silence.*

JERRY (*A new seriousness*): . . . You really have the rights?

AL: An *option* on the rights. But it's as good as set. Assuming you come through.

JERRY: You mean I'm like the deal-breaker here.

AL: No no, we'd get someone else. I'm just giving you first crack at this.

JERRY: How'd you get this thing?

AL: We're close friends of hers.

JERRY: *What?*

AL: That so weird?

JERRY: . . . Well . . .

AL: You don't think she has any friends? (*To LOU*) Biggest female rock star in like maybe the whole world and he doesn't think she has any friends!

JERRY (*Mounting suspicion*): Al—

AL: You want proof of my sincerity.

JERRY: I think I would like that. Yes. Not that—

AL (*To LOU*): Gimme the knife.

LOU: Al—

AL grabs the knife.

AL (*To JERRY*): This is for you, momser! (*He looks at his wrists*)

JERRY: Al—

LOU: Your wrists just healed!

AL: I'll cut where there aren't scars. (*He starts to slice his wrists*)

JERRY: Al, this is completely unnecessary.

AL: And I'm gonna drip on your fuckin' shoes! (*He starts dripping blood on JERRY's shoes*) How's that for sincerity?

JERRY: Al, this is very childish.

AL: When I give my word to a friend, I give my word.

JERRY: Fine. I believe!

AL: I can stop bleeding now?

JERRY: Please.

AL (*Wrapping up his wrists*): Eat the napkin.

JERRY: Al—

AL: You slash your wrists, you won't eat a paper napkin? Eat the fuckin' napkin! It's symbolic!

JERRY: Of what?

AL: Of your hunger for this deal. (*JERRY sighs, picks up the napkin, puts it in his mouth, chews it. Keeps chewing. With effort, swallows it. Opens his mouth. AL and LOU inspect*) Good.

LOU (*To AL*): Still not convinced he really cares.

JERRY: I will not cut my wrists again!

AL: Not asking that.

JERRY (*Menacing*): Al—

AL (*To LOU*): Let's assume he cares.

JERRY: Thank you.

AL: *For the moment only.* Zoom ahead to night. Any plans?

JERRY: Tonight? Uhhhh no.

AL: Once it's dark—I'm figuring now you're on the team—the three of us will leave for the house of the woman whose name you just ate.

JERRY (*Stunned*): . . . She's *expecting* us?

AL: She is.

JERRY: I mean . . . like me, *too*?

AL: You, too.

LOU: Al's described you to her.

AL: In glowing terms.

JERRY: God.

AL: And if she takes a shine to you, we close the deal tonight.

LOU: *Consummatus est.*

AL: Lou used to be a nun. (*JERRY stares at her in shock. AL picks up a tiny bell*) So. How hungry are you, Jer? How much does this all mean to you? (*He rings the bell*) We've got to know. (*RAMÓN enters carrying a silver tray with a silver bowl covered by a silver lid, sets it down in front of*

JERRY, and leaves. JERRY stares at the bowl) . . . You do want in?

JERRY: Of course.

AL: Why?

JERRY: Well, it's . . . so big.

AL: Not good enough.

JERRY: A lot of money can be made.

AL: You're wasting our fuckin' time.

LOU: Get rid of him.

JERRY: Al—!

AL: Get out.

JERRY: What the hell is going on?

AL: You say a thing like that to me, what am I to make of it? Jesus, man. You're like fuckin' dead. (*To LOU, mockingly*) "A lot of money can be made."

JERRY: It can't?

AL: Fuck you!

JERRY: I did not come here—

AL: Hey! You came here for whatever I could give you. And I'm giving you back your life. This is what I get?

JERRY: I don't know what the fuck you're talking about!

AL: This is more than money! A lot more! Fuck the money!

LOU: Fuck the money!

AL: Once upon a time you had the fire, man! You had the THING!

JERRY: Fuck you.

AL: There we go.

JERRY: I don't need this shit.

AL: There we go, there we go, now we're getting there! (*To LOU*) He's getting there!

JERRY: What the fuck is going on?

AL: Shove the money up your ass.

LOU: Right.

AL: I mean, if that's all you're in this for.

JERRY: I'm NOT!

AL: Then what?

JERRY: For . . .

AL: What? *What?*

JERRY: The excitement?

AL (*To LOU, in disbelief*): "The excitement."

JERRY: Yeah!

AL: You're fuckin' dead.

JERRY: Al—

AL: Your wife blows her brains out, and you're the one who's dead.

JERRY: What!?

AL: I read the trades, man. You think I don't know what's what!?

JERRY: I'm getting out.

AL: Hey! Best news I've heard! Go. Get out! Your fuckin' wife kills herself, and you're like this? Like *this*? Get out o' here. When you get home, slit your fuckin' wrists for real, dc something useful with your life! You're a fuckin' disgrace. (*JERRY goes for AL. AL knees him. JERRY falls*) Fuckin pathetic. (*To LOU*) He used to be somethin' else.

JERRY: You sonofabitch.

AL: What else is new?

JERRY: I shoulda fuckin' killed you.

AL: Sure. Right. You and what army? Your wife killed herself because being bored to death with you was just too fuckin' slow. (*JERRY goes for AL again. Again AL wins*) I gave you a chance to come back! To redeem yourself! To find the spark of life again! To be *involved*! I mean, with something big! Something that takes balls! We've got the biggest fuckin' rock star in the world, crazy as a loon, her life, she's like in amnesia, an audience just waiting, I mean, talk about your challenges, to bring this off . . .

LOU: It's a waste of time.

JERRY (*Grasping at straws*): Is her story any good?

Stunned pause.

AL: . . . *What?*

JERRY: Is her life story any good?

AL: In what way?

JERRY: Does it hold up?

Beat.

AL: . . . To what?

JERRY: Scrutiny.

AL stares at JERRY, incredulous.

AL: Does it hold up to fuckin' *scrutiny?*

JERRY: Yeah.

AL (*Menacingly*): You making fun of me?

JERRY: No!

LOU: Al—

AL (*Hushing LOU with a gesture*): You wanna know if her story holds up to scrutiny.

JERRY: If I come in on this, I have to know what I'm getting into.

LOU (*Sotto voce*): Ditch the creep.

AL *signals to* LOU *to keep quiet. He ponders the issue. Beat.*

AL: I would say it holds up quite well to scrutiny.

JERRY: That's good.

AL (*To* LOU, *sotto voce*): Unbelievable. (*To* JERRY) So what else you wanna know?

JERRY: What's up on the screen?

AL: Whatever we decide to put there.

Pause.

JERRY: But it's her *life*.

AL: Right. And the woman can't remember what she did.

Pause.

JERRY: . . . What?

AL: She's a fuckin' ditz-head. I mean, she's a sweetheart, please don't get me wrong. It's just that little specks of white dusty stuff have channeled, through the years, from one nostril to the other, and back through here, and down into here, and up into here, and here. Bong her on the head, she resonates.

JERRY: So what's she written?

AL: I've shown you. *Moby Dick.*

JERRY: Come on.

AL: I'm telling you. She's written fuckin' *Moby Dick.*

JERRY: Word for word?

AL: By and large.

JERRY: Al—

AL: SHE COPIED FUCKIN' *MOBY DICK!* Scrawl, scrawl, scribble, scribble. Okay?

JERRY: Wha'd she think she was doing?

AL: Keeping busy, I dunno. She claims it's her life story.

JERRY: Well, she's nuts.

AL: Who's arguing?

JERRY: God.

AL: She doesn't think her fans have read *Moby Dick*.

LOU: I never heard of it till today.

AL: You see? (*JERRY stares off, stunned*) To make her life story more personal, she changed Ahab's name to hers.

JERRY: And made Moby Dick a cock.

AL: Right.

LOU: Moby Dick's not a cock?

JERRY: It's a WHALE!

LOU: A cock's more interesting.

AL: I agree. (*To JERRY*) How many producers would let you work on a project like this?

JERRY: Al—

AL: My pleasure. Anyway, when we meet with her tonight, don't mention Melville's name.

JERRY: Why's she doing this?

AL: She wants the world to know her story.

JERRY: So she writes *Moby Dick*?

AL: Now you see why we don't want this falling into enemy hands.

JERRY stares off, puzzled. JERRY turns to AL.

JERRY: You ever seen one of her concerts?

AL: I go all the time.

JERRY: Then you know.

AL: . . . What?

JERRY: She's like a great fuckin' performer. This doesn't compute.

AL: In what way?

JERRY: She's in complete control up there. Every single moment. Absolute command. Knows exactly what she's doing!

AL: Right. That's *onstage*.

JERRY: So?

AL: Onstage, she's in a world she can handle. (*JERRY stares at AL. Beat. Then he looks away, clearly upset*) Hey. This film's her idea. If we don't produce it, someone else will.

JERRY (*Darkly suspicious*): How'd you get hold of this?

AL: I told you. We're like very close friends.

JERRY: And how'd *that* happen?

AL: To tell you would transgress the bonds of our friendship.

JERRY: Bullshit.

AL: Jerry, this woman is ferociously loyal to her friends and expects no less back. 'Nuf said.

LOU (*To AL, sotto voce*): I don't trust this guy.

AL: I'm handling this! (*To JERRY*) So are you in or out?

JERRY: Something's weird.

AL: Her head is what's weird.

LOU: Cut bait now.

AL: *I'm handling this!* Jer, what's wrong?

JERRY: I don't know.

AL: You've been out of touch too long, that's what's wrong.

JERRY: Maybe.

AL: No maybe, *yes.* Let me sweeten the pot. Whet your appetite a bit. You ready? She's agreed to appear in the film.

JERRY: . . . Can she act?

AL: *Jerry!*

JERRY: Sorry.

AL: Jerry, to be crass for just a moment, if I may . . . I know money's not your prime concern, nor mine, but it's close. I estimate we are looking at roughly anything from our own personal Fort Knox to King Solomon's Mine apiece. That's you, me, and Lou, and that's in the first week only. So much for financial satisfaction. What about "artistic" satisfaction? . . . Jerry, what do you think the captains of the film industry will say when this film that you, Lou, and I have independently produced is released? They will say, *"How come we didn't get this fucker OURSELVES!?"* When's the last time you've had that kind of artistic satisfaction? (*JERRY ponders*) Now I would like to interject a philosophical note. Jerry, someday my name, like yours, like Lou's, will be writ in the big prompt book in the sky. Assuming it has an index, under what specific category do you think I most expect to find my name?

JERRY: . . . Asshole?

AL (*To LOU*): Is this guy somethin' or is he somethin'? (*To JERRY*) Putz! I'm serious! What category of personage will I have been? What will posterity know me for?

JERRY: Doing good?

AL: Jesus!

JERRY: What's wrong with doin' good?

AL: Nothin'! I am talking about as an *achievement*. My grand-
mother did good. Knitted for the blind. You want your grave-
stone to say "He knitted for the blind"? (*JERRY shakes his
head no*) So, what have I set my sights on? What is the single
greatest driving force of my life?

JERRY: It used to be staying out of jail.

AL: And that is still a major driving force, no question, but it's
not what I dream of being known for when I die. "Here lies
Al Sereno. He stayed out of jail." I mean, what the fuck kind
of ambition is that? That's fuckin' rat shit!

JERRY: I give up.

AL: Making my mark. (*JERRY stares at AL, startled*) I want to
make my fuckin' MARK! I wanna put my fuckin' footprint
down *in the sands of TIME!* That's what I want. *And I bet
anything you do, too.* (*JERRY seems shaken*) Jer, with this
film, Us and History will be wed! We will leave our footprints
in the fuckin' sands of time with this! (*JERRY begins to nod.
A faint trace of a smile appears*) You know what I dream?
Like every night? The future has arrived. We're like a cen-
tury down the line. And some—what?—he digs up bones.

JERRY: Graverobber.

AL: More scientific.

JERRY: Anthropologist.

AL: That's it! Some anthropologist looks down upon the soil of
this fair earth and says, "Behold! I know that print! *Al Sereno
walked here.*" And people will know what he means by that.
And they'll build a fence around that meager, dusty footprint. And charge money to gaze at it. *And people will PAY!*
(*JERRY smiles. AL sees the smile*) I know you so fuckin' well!

It's your dream, too! Has to be! Could I love someone who didn't dream like me?

JERRY: Sarah thought I'd lost the dream.

AL: Well, you hadn't!

JERRY: I was what was lost.

AL: Right now, I have a feeling that sweet wonderful ex-wife of yours is smiling down.

JERRY: I hope.

AL: I *know*! So. You in or out?

JERRY: I'm in.

AL: Lemme hear.

JERRY: I'm in!

AL: Say "I want in."

JERRY: I want in!

AL: Louder.

JERRY: I WANT IN!

AL: *Now* you're comin' through. Tell me why.

JERRY: It's obvious.

AL: To me. I'm still not sure for you, and I've gotta be.

JERRY: Well, it's out of sight.

AL: What I can't see I don't know.

JERRY: It's like a dream come true.

AL: That I know. Good. In what way?

JERRY: Well. To get a thing like this, to be the ones I mean to have *gotten* it . . .

AL: What?

JERRY: . . . Well, think how everybody *else* will feel.

AL: There we go!

JERRY: I mean, talk about envy—

AL: Jealousy!

JERRY: Hatred! Blind fuckin' hatred! Yes!

AL: And yet?

JERRY: Love.

AL: Not love.

JERRY: *Feigned* love.

AL: FEIGNED!

JERRY: Which is even better.

AL: Why?

JERRY: You can bank feigned love.

AL: Feigned love gives dividends!

JERRY: Real love breaks hearts.

AL: Causes heartburn.

JERRY: Real love sucks hind tit!

AL: Good. What else?

JERRY (*Stronger*) *What else?* Whatever deal you want after this
    is *YOURS!*

AL: There you go!

JERRY: Anything you want, if it *exists*, is yours.

AL: What if it does not exist?

JERRY: God will see that it is *made* to exist.

AL: That's right. *Because* . . . ?

JERRY: You're king.

AL: Who's king?

JERRY: We're king.

AL: WE'RE king!

JERRY: All of us are king.

AL: All of us! Me an' you an' Lou!

JERRY: And we'll get things then . . .

AL: Say it, Jer.

JERRY: We will get things then . . .

AL: Go on. What sort of things? Say it, Jer, go on!

JERRY: We will get things then that none of us ever even dared
to dream of!

AL: There you go! Never even dared to *dream* of! That is what
we'll get!

LOU: *Things we never even dared to dream of!*

JERRY: I think maybe we were born for this.

AL: We were!

LOU: I've somehow always known we were.

JERRY: What it is . . . it's the fucking *culmination*! (AL *turns to*
LOU *and smiles.* JERRY *is staring out, lost in dreams*) When
everything makes sense.

AL *reaches over and removes the lid from the silver bowl in front
of* JERRY. JERRY *is first made aware of what's in front of him by
smell. Apparently, it stinks.*

AL: How hungry are you, Jer? (JERRY *stares at the bowl in
perplexity and then revulsion. What's inside resembles
chili*) How much do you really *want* to be king?

JERRY: . . . This is *shit.*

AL: But not *ordinary* shit.

JERRY: *What*?

AL: Ordinary shit can make you sick. That's not our intention here. This is special shit.

JERRY (*In shock, numb*): *Special* shit.

AL: *Very* special shit.

JERRY: You've given me a bowl of very special *shit*?

AL: Jerry—

JERRY: To *eat*?

AL: Just one spoon.

JERRY: I don't fuckin' believe this.

AL: Jerry, look—

JERRY: I'm looking! This is what you meant by "Come for lunch"?

AL: Jerry, please . . .

JERRY: Please what? Please eat? Five years ago, you ruined my career, that wasn't good enough?

AL: Jer, what we're after is symbolic.

JERRY: I see! This is *symbolic* shit!

AL: Right.

JERRY: Symbolic of SHIT!

AL: Jer—

JERRY: You fuckin' drove my wife to suicide!

AL: That's unfair!

JERRY: You're telling *me* it was unfair!? Where's the fuckin' knife?

AL: Jer—

JERRY: Shoulda fuckin' done it when I first thought of it!

AL: Jerry, LISTEN! This is not intended as an insult.

JERRY: Well, it's not exactly flattering!

AL: Jerry—!

JERRY: My ego is like nonexistent! I'm a shattered man, my wife is dead, my life is done, you invite me to lunch and feed me shit? I mean, Jesus, Al! how do you think that makes me *feel*?

AL: Jerry, it's a test!

JERRY: Of whether I kill you first or myself!

AL: No!

JERRY: Yes!

AL: Jerry, listen—*I love you, man.*

JERRY: I don't fuckin' believe this!

AL: Would I have you here if I didn't!? This is a *test*!

JERRY (*Mimicking a PA system*): "This is a test!"

AL: We've got to know that we can count on you in the crunch!

JERRY: So you want me to eat shit.

AL (*Calm*): Jerry . . .

JERRY: If we put this in a film no one would believe it.

AL: Jerry, listen—

JERRY: A writer of fiction would not go *near* what is going on here today!

AL: Jerry, this is not ordinary shit!

JERRY: I heard you, Al. It's not a comfort.

AL: Would I give you ordinary shit?

JERRY: Never! I know that! Believe me! It's about the only thing left I really know!

AL: Jerry, this . . . is nun shit.

JERRY: . . . *Nun* shit?

AL: It comes from nuns.

JERRY: *Nuns!?*

AL: Exclusively.

JERRY: I don't fuckin' believe this.

AL: Cross my heart.

JERRY: This bowl of shit . . .

AL: Exclusively from nuns.

JERRY: *Pure* nun shit.

AL: *Pure* nun shit!

JERRY: You think I'm a fuckin' ASS?

AL: Jer—

JERRY: I have SOME BRAINS LEFT!

AL: Jer—

JERRY: You expect me to believe this shit comes from nuns?

AL: May God strike me dead.

JERRY: Al, I have heard of nuns selling . . . jam.

AL: We didn't pay for this.

JERRY: You mean they're just *giving* it away?

AL: I mean one cannot BUY this stuff!

JERRY: I'd think not!

AL: *Lou* got the stuff. (*JERRY stares at LOU*) . . . She still has connections.

LOU smiles proudly.

JERRY: Holy shit.

AL (*Apologetic*): It's as close as we could get.

JERRY: Oh, Jesus.

AL: Jer, we need a sign.

JERRY (*Frightened now*): Sign?

LOU: One little sign.

AL: We need to know that we can count on you.

JERRY: No!

AL: Jer—

JERRY: No! I'm sorry! NO!

AL: Jer, it's not as bad as you think.

JERRY: Then *you* eat!

LOU: We already have.

JERRY: . . . When you cut your wrists.

AL and LOU (*Together*): Right.

JERRY moans.

AL: Jer. One spoon. That's all we ask.

LOU: It's a symbol.

AL: We have to know you can be counted on.

LOU (*Sweet, gentle smile*): One spoon.

AL: Not half as bad as you think.

LOU: Really.

AL: Just one little spoon.

LOU: *One spoon for the kingdom.*

AL: One spoon *or you're out.*

AL picks up the spoon and holds it out to JERRY. JERRY *stares at the spoon. Fade to black.*

ACT TWO

In the dark, we hear music. It's the vamp to NIRVANA's *"Who I Am," a pop song with a strong, driving beat. A moment later, we hear the voice of a radio disc jockey. As he talks, the music fades a bit.*

DJ: It's about fifteen minutes past the hour. Case you haven't noticed, it's starting to get a little dark out there. And coming up, right now, to bring on the night, we've got Nirvana—who else could it be?—fourteen weeks at the top of the charts, at number one, and here she is with "Who I Am"!

The music comes back in with NIRVANA *singing.*

I've got nothing to hide
Nothing's denied
There's nothing you can't view.
I'll take no blame
I feel no shame
For doin' all the things I do.

Some people say what I do is crazy
But I just do what they dream.

> *This is it! Who I am!*
> *I am everything you want me to be.*
> *This is it! Who I am!*
> *Come inside of me.*

*Lights up slightly. Moonlight illumines what seems to be some
kind of pagan temple with a grand staircase. Tropical foliage is
all around.*

  *A woman is standing in the shadows, surveying the area. One
can sense power in this woman, just from the way she stands.
It's* NIRVANA, *making sure everything is in order.*

  The song continues uninterrupted.

I'm a mirror of your life.
I'm your mistress, your lover, your wife.
Give me time, I'll make you see
Why who you are is me.
Some people say I'm a bad moon rising
But I'm just the mirror of you.

  This is it! Who I am!
  I am everything you want me to be.
  This is it! Who I am!
  Come inside of me.

A man's voice is suddenly heard on a PA system.

VOICE ON PA SYSTEM: They're here.

NIRVANA *goes to a control box. A speaker system is inside.*

NIRVANA: Send them down.

She strolls off. The music ends. A few moments later, LOU *appears
at the top of the grand stairs.*

LOU: Watch your step.

JERRY *and* AL *descend behind her.*

JERRY (*Peering into the shadows*): . . . What is this, the
  Parthenon?

AL: Close. Lou, go hit the lights.

LOU moves off into the shadows and over to the control box.

JERRY (*Nervously*): How come we're not meeting up at her house?

AL: 'Cause she wants to meet down here. (*JERRY looks about nervously*) Hey, relax. You're gonna do fine.

LOU flicks a switch in the control box. One by one, the lights of NIRVANA's amazing swimming pool come on, all accompanied by seraphic music.

JERRY: Oh my God!

The place looks like the Grand Temple of Karnak combined with a bit of Uxmal. [Note: we cannot actually see the pool—it's at a lower level.] The edifice is on several levels. AL and JERRY are on the top. From here, the grand staircase sweeps down to a deck with lounge chairs fit for a pharaoh.

AL: Jerry, in my humble estimation, this is what a swimming pool should look like.

JERRY descends in awe. He walks to the edge of the pool and stares out as if he were seeing God.

JERRY: *Jesus . . . !*

AL comes over to JERRY.

AL: You don't get this doing educational films, remember that. Whatever happens.

JERRY: Al, I've gotta tell you—I'm really scared.

AL: You're gonna do fine. Lou, go get him a drink.

LOU goes for some champagne that's in a small bar nearby.

JERRY: But what if I screw up?

AL: You won't.

JERRY: But let's just say I *do.*

AL: Hey! Have you got ears? You're gonna do *fine.* Now relax. We wouldn't have brought you if we didn't have total confidence. (*To LOU*) Right?

LOU has returned with three glasses of champagne.

LOU: Right.

She hands JERRY and AL glasses. They raise their glasses in a toast.
As they do, NIRVANA appears in the shadows at the periphery, a hand over her face. She studies JERRY. JERRY notices her. NIRVANA exits, hand over her face.

JERRY: Was that . . . ?

AL: Nirvana. Yeah.

JERRY: Something wrong with her face?

AL: Uh-uh.

LOU: She just doesn't trust you yet.

JERRY: . . . Trust me?

AL: Nirvana's face is very . . . *private.*

LOU: Probably the most private part of her entire body.

AL: Right.

LOU: She reveals it only to her closest friends.

JERRY: . . . But . . .

AL: On *stage?*

JERRY: Yeah.

AL: That's not her face.

JERRY: . . . What?

AL: That's her *public* face.

JERRY: But . . .

LOU: It's different.

AL: Don't ask how.

LOU: Just is.

JERRY: Holy shit.

AL: Hey! Stay calm! Staying calm is the key.

LOU: Really. She *smells* fear.

JERRY takes a few deep breaths, trying to relax. NIRVANA enters, a veil across the lower part of her face.

NIRVANA (*To AL*): What's his name?

AL (*To JERRY, beneath his breath*): Tell her your name.

JERRY: Jerry.

She ponders.

NIRVANA: We'll have to find something better.

AL: Anything you say.

NIRVANA: How's Janet?

AL (*To JERRY*): You feel comfortable with Janet?

JERRY: No.

NIRVANA: *No?*

AL (*To JERRY, sotto voce*): Say yes.

JERRY: No!

NIRVANA: I like that. He has balls! (*To LOU*) Is that on his
    résumé?

LOU: That he has balls?

NIRVANA: Yes.

LOU: Did we bring a résumé?

AL: I'm afraid we didn't bring a résumé. (*To JERRY, sotto voce*)
    You're doing fine.

JERRY gives AL a look; JERRY is not so sure.

NIRVANA (*To JERRY*): You ever worked in features?

AL: Of course he's worked in features! He's worked with me. I
  wept the day he said, "Al, forgive me, but I've gotta leave."

NIRVANA (*To JERRY*): Why'd you leave?

AL (*To JERRY, quickly*): Lemme tell. (*To NIRVANA*) The man is
  too modest. "Why did he leave?" He left because he felt the
  pull of a higher calling. (*JERRY, interested in what's coming
  next, turns and stares at AL*) This man made a vow to his
  beloved dying wife that he would turn his astounding genius,
  after she departed, to the bettering of the uneducated world.
  She . . . had been uneducated . . . until she met him.

NIRVANA (*To JERRY, in astonishment*): Where did she grow up?

JERRY turns to AL for help.

AL: She was raised by wolves.

NIRVANA stares at JERRY in awe.

NIRVANA: *Wow.*

JERRY shrugs modestly.

AL (*To NIRVANA*): We are going to do *her* life story after we do
  yours.

NIRVANA: I like this man *very much.*

AL: Of course. That's why I brought him here. I said to Lou,
  "Honey, for this project, we are gonna need the *best!*"

NIRVANA studies JERRY. JERRY smiles back proudly. Suddenly NIRVANA turns to LOU with a look of great distress.

NIRVANA (*Softly, desperate*): Lou, I'm runnin' low.

LOU: I'll have 'em by tomorrow.

NIRVANA: I can't wait.

LOU: How's late tonight?

NIRVANA: How late?

LOU: . . . Two?

NIRVANA: Shit.

LOU: I'll try for one.

NIRVANA: I wouldn't ask if, like—

LOU: I'll have it here by one.

NIRVANA: What if you can't?

LOU (*Warm, comforting, loving*): Hey! This is my problem now. Not yours. Okay? Relax.

NIRVANA goes over to LOU and hugs her. LOU hugs her back.

NIRVANA (*Whispers*) I could also use—

LOU: That I've got with me.

NIRVANA smiles.

NIRVANA (*To AL and JERRY*): Be right back. (*She and LOU exit*)

JERRY: So. You're back dealing drugs.

AL: *Drugs?*

JERRY: Hey!

AL: I was never in drugs.

JERRY: *Never in drugs!*

AL: Never! *Never!* But I understand why you think I was.

JERRY: 'Cause you were.

AL: Not for profit. *Never for profit!* . . . For me, it was like a calling. I gave to friends, Jerry, friends in *need.* I was like the Ford Foundation. Drugs are a curse, man, a fuckin' curse.

JERRY: So you're not in drugs anymore.

AL: Absolutely out of it. I am one thing only—I am an independent fuckin' film producer!

JERRY: I don't believe you.

AL: All right. Okay. Those were drugs.

JERRY: That's great.

AL: You think I'm proud?

JERRY: Yeah!

AL: I am! We *both* are! Jerry, that woman cannot walk out on a fuckin' stage without our help! We are the glue that holds her together! We are her *protectors*! Jerry, outside this house, there are snakes waiting to get at her. They were in here *with* her till we came and got rid of them. You understand what I'm saying here? (*JERRY shakes his head*) I am saying, without *us*, Jerry, she is even worse off than this. *Compassion*, man. That woman needs our support.

JERRY stares at AL. LOU and NIRVANA return.

NIRVANA (*To AL*): If I ever hear that you've done dirt of any sort to this sainted fuckin' woman, I will have you torn apart, physically torn apart. You understand?

AL: What the fuck has brought *this* on?

NIRVANA (*To LOU*): If he ever does anything to you that you don't like, I mean *anything*, you come and tell me right away. I want you to promise.

AL: Hey!

NIRVANA: This woman is too good for you.

AL: Come on!

NIRVANA: You don't think she is?

AL: That isn't what I mean.

NIRVANA (*To LOU*): Does he love you?

LOU: I dunno.

AL: *What!?*

LOU (*To NIRVANA*): He *says* he does.

AL: Oh my God.

LOU (*With obvious uncertainty*): I think he does.

AL: Of course I do!

NIRVANA: So how come she isn't sure?

AL: 'Cause she's a ditz!

NIRVANA: I don't like that kind of talk!

AL: I'm sorry. Lou?—I love you. Okay?

NIRVANA: *Don't ever fuck with me or the people that I love!*

AL: I'm not! I wouldn't dream of it! How can you even *think* such a thing? (*NIRVANA stares at him suspiciously*) . . . And I love you, too. (*Beat*) The same goes for Jerry.

NIRVANA: . . . His name is Jerry?

AL: His name is Jerry.

NIRVANA (*To LOU*): Should I show him my face?

LOU: Would you . . . *like* to?

NIRVANA: Only if he really wants to see it.

LOU: Ask him.

NIRVANA (*To JERRY*): Wanna see my face?

JERRY: . . . Only if you want.

NIRVANA: If I do, who will you tell?

JERRY: If you don't want me to tell anyone, I won't tell anyone.

NIRVANA: Blood oath? (*JERRY holds out his bandaged wrists*) No
  need. (*To AL and LOU*) He's good! (*To JERRY*) Okay. I'm
  going to let you see my face. (*To AL and LOU*) Hide your
  eyes.

*AL and LOU shade their eyes. NIRVANA lifts her veil. The sight
takes JERRY's breath away.*

JERRY: I can't tell you what this means.

NIRVANA: Would you like to . . . *kiss* my face?

JERRY: . . . Where?

NIRVANA: Anywhere.

JERRY: Does that include . . . your lips?

NIRVANA: If you wish. (*JERRY kisses her tentatively on the lips.
  It's a brief kiss. Chaste. He pulls back and stares at her*)
  . . . What did you think?

JERRY: I thought . . . millions upon millions of people *dream*
  . . . about what I have just done.

NIRVANA: Would you call it . . . "sufficient"?

JERRY: You mean, I can kiss you *again*?

NIRVANA: If you like.

AL (*To LOU, sotto voce*): This is unbelievable.

LOU (*Sotto voce*): Unbelievable.

JERRY (*To NIRVANA*): I'd like.

NIRVANA: Then do. (*He moves closer to her lips. Then he stops*)
. . . What?

JERRY: Can I put my tongue in your mouth?

NIRVANA (*To AL and LOU*): He's got guts! (*To JERRY*) Not yet
. . . Maybe tomorrow.

JERRY (*Overwhelmed*): . . . That—(*Pause*) I'm . . . (*Pause*) Thank
you. (*He kisses her passionately*)

NIRVANA (*To AL and LOU, after it's over*): Now you can look.
(*They look at her face reverently. To JERRY, re AL and LOU*)
They've seen it before.

AL: But always with such pleasure!

NIRVANA (*To JERRY, with a laugh*): I know it's a silly thing! I
mean, what am I guarding?

JERRY: It's not silly at all!

NIRVANA (*Hopeful look*): You don't think?

JERRY: No!

That one word takes her breath away. She stares at him. Pause.

NIRVANA: Somehow, I feel like we've just made love.

JERRY: The same.

NIRVANA: Why?

JERRY: . . . *Why?*

NIRVANA: There's no need to be afraid.

JERRY: I'm not!

NIRVANA: Then . . . ?

Pause.

JERRY: Well, we've been so *intimate.*

NIRVANA (*Moved*): Yes.

JERRY: It's *like* we made love.

NIRVANA: Yes!

JERRY: And yet . . .

NIRVANA: What?

JERRY: . . . In some odd way, *more* intimate.

NIRVANA: Than if we'd fucked?

JERRY: In a sense. I mean . . .

NIRVANA: Anyone can fuck.

JERRY: Yes.

NIRVANA: But not everyone can see my face *this close.*

JERRY: Right!

NIRVANA: You did.

JERRY: . . . Yes.

NIRVANA: I *let* you.

JERRY (*Moved*): I know.

NIRVANA: I gave you my *trust*.

JERRY: A most cherished prize.

NIRVANA: Yes. Yes. I give very few my trust.

JERRY: . . . What about your body?

NIRVANA: You want it?

JERRY (*Taken aback, but the answer is yes*): . . . Well . . .

NIRVANA: Just tell me if you do. 'Cause I don't care. It's not really mine. I'm just like, you know, *visiting*.

JERRY: . . . Visiting?

LOU: Nirvana is extremely old.

NIRVANA: I am over four thousand years old!

LOU: Nirvana has come back to earth many times.

NIRVANA: It's why I don't fear death.

JERRY: . . . Ah.

LOU (*To NIRVANA, re JERRY*): Can I say?

NIRVANA: Of course! We've just become *lovers*.

LOU: Nirvana is the reincarnation of Hopsepsut, Nefertiti's sister, concubine of Amenhotep and rightful ruler of the Eighteenth Dynasty.

JERRY doesn't know what to think.

NIRVANA: It's why so many of my fans believe they can see a divine and timeless spirit inside of me.

LOU: You have a *presence.*

NIRVANA: There! That's it. The *spark* accounts for where I am.

JERRY: Ah.

NIRVANA: A spark that has been passed down through the centuries like a "sacred torch"! Lou showed me this. Before Lou came I was really very deeply fucked up. (*To Lou*) Would you say that's right?

LOU (*To JERRY*): She was a mess.

NIRVANA: A mess! Fortunately, she *saw* something. Lou knows the stars. Lou can see things others can't. And she saw, in my eyes . . . (*She turns to LOU*) What was it?

LOU: Pyramids.

NIRVANA: Pyramids! Jutting up from the sands of time.

LOU: The Nile.

NIRVANA: The Nile! She saw the Nile! And I was singing . . . *Where?*

LOU: . . . At a party?

NIRVANA: I don't think so.

LOU: I can't remember.

NIRVANA: You *told* me!

LOU: Wait. Was it on a boat?

NIRVANA: I'm not sure.

LOU: Yes. A boat! The royal boat! I can see lots of oars. You're standing by the Pharaoh's side, and you're singing!

NIRVANA studies LOU. A pause. NIRVANA turns to JERRY.

NIRVANA: So then I knew, and I wasn't worried anymore.

JERRY: That's really great.

NIRVANA: *Helpful.*

JERRY: Very helpful.

NIRVANA: Very, very helpful. (*She glances at LOU. Then she takes hold of her veil*) I think I'm going to put this up again. I feel more comfortable. (*She lifts her veil*) Not that I don't trust you all. (*To AL and LOU*) I'd like to be alone with him now, if I could.

AL: Sure.

LOU: We'll go take a walk.

AL and LOU start out, AL flashing JERRY a thumbs-up sign as they leave. NIRVANA watches them go. As soon as they're gone, she turns to JERRY and removes her veil. Pause.

NIRVANA: Have you got any coke?

JERRY: I don't—uhhhhh—*do* coke.

She stares at him, stunned.

NIRVANA: . . . Why?

JERRY: Just . . . (*He shrugs*)

NIRVANA: Al doesn't get you stuff? (*JERRY shakes his head no*)
Lou got me Al.

JERRY: Ah.

NIRVANA: Lou gets me better stuff than Al. Al cuts his shit with
something that like fucks up my sinuses. I can't mess with
it when I sing.

JERRY: You're gonna kill yourself.

NIRVANA: I'll be reborn.

JERRY: You believe that?

NIRVANA: Do you?

He studies her.

JERRY (*Finally—soft, straight*): No.

NIRVANA: . . . So you don't think I'm the reincarnation of
Hopsepsut?

Pause.

JERRY: It's hard to say.

She stares off.

NIRVANA: It is.

JERRY studies her. Long pause.

JERRY (*Finally*): You really want to do this film?

NIRVANA: . . . Which?

JERRY: The story of your life.

NIRVANA: You mean *Moby Dick*!

JERRY: Yeah.

She ponders.

NIRVANA: If I tell you something, will you keep it secret?

JERRY: Sure.

NIRVANA: That's not my life.

JERRY (*Feigning surprise as best he can*): . . . Hah!

NIRVANA: Al doesn't think it matters. He's probably right.

JERRY: Why not do *your* life, then?

NIRVANA: I can't remember what I've done.

JERRY: Have you tried?

NIRVANA: Every day! I'd like to know how I got here as much
    as anybody. (*Pause*) Tell me what you see.

JERRY: . . . Where?

NIRVANA: In my face.

JERRY: . . . Why?

NIRVANA: A test.

He stares into her face. He sees something that astonishes him.

JERRY (*Startled*): . . . You're *scared!*

NIRVANA: I am.

JERRY (*Still staring into her eyes*): But not of me . . . Don't know
who. Can't say. Just . . . *scared.*

NIRVANA: Is it Lou?

JERRY: . . . *Lou?*

NIRVANA: Yes. *Is it Lou?*

JERRY: . . . I don't know.

NIRVANA: Is it Al?

JERRY: I don't know.

NIRVANA: What else?

JERRY: . . . Why do you ask that about Lou and Al?

NIRVANA: Because I think they may be here to chew me up.
(*JERRY stares off. Clearly, he has been thrown by her re-
marks*) . . . Will you betray me, too?

JERRY: No one is going to betray you.

NIRVANA: You know how much money this film will make?

JERRY: If you don't want to do it, don't do it.

NIRVANA: It matters to my fans.

JERRY: To see a life that isn't yours?

NIRVANA: I don't think they care about such things.

JERRY: They just care about seeing you.

NIRVANA: I think.

JERRY: Why?

NIRVANA: Beats me. Sure isn't for my singing. I look awkward when I dance. My body's only fair. And my acting sucks.

JERRY: It's an unbeatable combination.

NIRVANA: Reincarnation is really the only thing that explains it. *But Lou didn't remember where I'd sung!* It was not on some stupid boat in the Nile, it was in a fuckin' TEMPLE! The temple of the SUN GOD, RA! Why do you think I built this thing?

JERRY: So she forgot.

NIRVANA: I think she made the whole thing up.

JERRY: Why?

NIRVANA: It got her *in*.

Pause.

JERRY: But maybe she didn't.

NIRVANA (*Skeptically*): Maybe she didn't—right. And maybe Al really *does* care about me, like he says. Right?

JERRY (*With sincerity*): I think he does.

NIRVANA looks at JERRY in a new way. Is it possible he's telling the truth?

NIRVANA: . . . Did you really work with him?

JERRY: Yeah.

NIRVANA: When?

JERRY: Ten years ago.

NIRVANA: And you left because your mother was attacked by *wolves?*

JERRY: It had nothing to do with wolves.

NIRVANA (*Suddenly remembers*): She was *raised* by wolves!

JERRY: It's only a rumor.

NIRVANA: You want some good advice? Don't deny it.

JERRY: Who's denying? Was I *there?*

NIRVANA: There ya go! For the press kit, I would like to play up your wolf heritage.

JERRY: Fine.

NIRVANA: Makes the team sound, you know, like very *special*.

JERRY: I understand.

NIRVANA: So why'd you two split?

JERRY: We had a fight.

NIRVANA: Over . . . ?

JERRY: A film we made, *The Roustabouts*.

NIRVANA: That made money.

JERRY: Yeah.

NIRVANA: . . . So?

JERRY: I told him I thought it was a piece of shit . . . Or something original like that.

NIRVANA: And afterwards?

JERRY: . . . *Afterwards*?

NIRVANA: When it was in profit.

JERRY: . . . What about it?

NIRVANA: What was your opinion then?

JERRY: That's when I told him.

She stares at him, flabbergasted.

NIRVANA: You told him it was a piece of shit when it was in *profit*?

JERRY: I know it's a difficult concept to accept.

NIRVANA: I'll say!

JERRY: Especially for Al. He decided my opinion was now obviously useless. So he fired me . . . And fucked my wife.

NIRVANA: That seems excessive.

JERRY: I thought so.

NIRVANA: . . . And that's why she died?

Pause.

JERRY: In a way.

Pause.

NIRVANA: So why are you working with him now?

JERRY: *You.*

She stares at him. Pause.

NIRVANA: Let's talk about this film. Jerry, earlier I said this script was really not the story of my life. Do you recall?

JERRY: Vividly!

NIRVANA: Well, in some odd way, I think it may really *be* my life. Do you understand what I mean by that?

JERRY: . . . No.

NIRVANA: That's because you're not thinking big enough.

JERRY: Okay.

NIRVANA: Jerry, in the grand scheme of things, details like where did I grow up or go to school, what do these things matter?

JERRY: . . . Because . . . you've been here for *centuries.*

NIRVANA: *CENTURIES!* Yes! Jerry, my life on this plane has been *nothing.* That's why I can't remember it. My *real* life— Jerry, that has been led on a wholly different *kind* of plane. But how does one *depict* that kind of plane?

JERRY: Very difficult.

NIRVANA: *Very* difficult! Except . . . ? (*She stares at him*)

JERRY: . . . Through . . . something . . . like *this.*

NIRVANA: YES! Jerry, I believe a Higher Force was at work when I wrote *Moby Dick.* A force that's been watching over me since the dawn of Time. Jerry, Al didn't bring you to me— the gods did.

JERRY: You know, I'm going to tell you something. This sounds weird—but when Al called me up and asked me to fly out here . . . ?

NIRVANA: You were surprised.

JERRY: *Totally!* And yet . . . ?

NIRVANA: In a way, you weren't.

JERRY: That's right! In a way, I've been *expecting* it.

NIRVANA: Jerry, I don't want to do this film unless it's on *that kind of level.*

JERRY: And you shouldn't.

NIRVANA: And you shouldn't either. *(Pause)* Okay, let's get specific: the great white cock—how big should it be?

JERRY: . . . Well—

NIRVANA: I've been thinking very *huge.*

JERRY: I would think.

NIRVANA: Huge enough for me to mount.

JERRY: . . . *Mount?*

NIRVANA: And ride.

JERRY: Like a . . .

NIRVANA: Whale. Okay, what sort of boat should I go after it in?

JERRY: . . . Rowboat?

NIRVANA: ROWBOAT! Good. And then this big cock just sort of . . . *(She gestures upward)*

JERRY: Emerges.

NIRVANA: Yes! And opens up its . . .

JERRY: . . . Mouth?

NIRVANA: No.

JERRY: Opening.

NIRVANA: "Opening"! Opens up its "opening." And *shoots!*

JERRY: I think that could be done.

NIRVANA: FLOODS THE BOAT! We're going down. I'm drowning in the stuff! Jerry, I've had nights like this, *nights!* (*Calm, business-like*) Now, to me, that's a very remarkable scene.

JERRY: In my opinion? No one's ever seen anything like it.

NIRVANA: Because no one's had the guts to tell it like it is. Jerry, this story speaks to everyone. Okay—the next thing I see? The thing ATTACKS! And tries to suck me in.

JERRY: The *cock?*

NIRVANA: Yes. Opens up its . . .

JERRY: Opening—

NIRVANA: —opening and . . . (*She makes the sounds of a giant vacuum cleaner*) . . . Could a cock do that, do you think?

JERRY: Hey! One that size? You could suck in refrigerators.

NIRVANA: God! . . . Okay. Somehow I get out. And regroup.

JERRY: Would you *kill* the cock?

NIRVANA: Eventually, I believe I would, I *MUST!*

JERRY: I would think.

NIRVANA: Maybe I even die.

JERRY: In the struggle.

NIRVANA: Yes! I can see that happening. To save the world from its sins, somehow I just . . . *take it in.*

JERRY: The cock?

NIRVANA: I just TAKE IT IN!

JERRY: That could be difficult.

NIRVANA: If it isn't difficult, why do it?

JERRY: You're right. You're absolutely right!

NIRVANA: Jerry, is this film any good?

Pause. JERRY stares out as if he's never heard of this concept.

JERRY: . . . Any *good?*

NIRVANA: Because I can imagine people saying it's not.

JERRY: Would that bother you?

NIRVANA: Not if I believed in it.

JERRY (*With alarm*): I thought you did!

NIRVANA: I'm not sure. Look, I'm being frank. I could go either way on this. If it's right for me, I'll know. *Is it any good?*

Pause.

JERRY: I would say that this film . . . the *idea* of it . . . (*He ponders*) . . . Well, it's just *beyond categorization.* It's just . . . (*Gesturing outward and upward, toward the heavens*) . . . *out* there. (*To her, with a smile*) . . . Like you. (*His eyes stay fixed on hers. She stares back. Finally . . .*)

NIRVANA: All right. Here's the deal. If you say to me, Nirvana, go with this film, I will go with it. And if you say, Don't, I won't. And if you sell me out, you're dead.

JERRY: I would never—!

NIRVANA: HEY! Of course you would. *No one fucks with me!* (*JERRY stares at her, stunned*) But they sure like to try. Even Lou. *Christ!* Hey. That's all right. Keeps me on my guard. I can handle it. No one gets into bed with me for nothing unless I say so, and this is not one of those times.

JERRY: I don't know what you're talking about.

NIRVANA: Sure you do. I am giving you three fuckers a big free ride with this. I am your gravy train to fame and fortune. I know when I'm being had. And I will expect some equivalent compensation.

JERRY: You don't have to worry about me!

NIRVANA: You think I'm a fuckin' idiot? Al does. I'm not. I know Melville wrote *Moby Dick*. Fuck 'm! Al gets me things I need, and he's not as greedy as the others used to be when he fucks me over. (*Calls*) AL!? LOU!? (*Back to JERRY*) Everyone thinks I'm theirs for the taking. That's okay. In a way I am. I'm used to it by now. I've learned how to protect myself. *I take back.* (*AL and LOU enter. They stop and stare toward NIRVANA and JERRY. To AL and LOU*) I think he's gonna do just fine. (*They smile with relief. NIRVANA takes JERRY aside, out of earshot*) It's all up to you. You say the film's a go, we go. If it's a go, we'll talk terms. I'll wait for your answer over there. *You're my protector now.* (*She puts her veil back over her face and exits, past AL and LOU*)

LOU: . . . What's happened?

JERRY: I'm not sure.

LOU and AL exchange uneasy looks.

AL: . . . Well wha'd she say?

JERRY: This and that.

AL: . . . She said this and that?

JERRY: Yeah.

AL (*To LOU*): She ever say anything like that to you?

LOU: Never.

AL: Me neither. Jerry, *what the fuck's going on?*

JERRY: We've got a go-ahead if I say yes.

AL: . . . If *you* say yes?

JERRY: At the moment, she seems to trust me a bit more than either one of you.

LOU: *What?*

AL: Fuck that! Deal's off!

LOU: Al!

AL: You're right. That's a stupid thing to say. (*Brightening on the instant*) Well! This is good news.

JERRY: For who?

Beat.

AL: . . . For *who*? For all of us!

JERRY (*Trace of a smile*): Not necessarily.

AL and LOU stare at JERRY with a sudden foreboding.

AL and LOU (*Together*): What?

JERRY: Al, Lou, I don't know how to tell you this . . . But I'm not sure if I should keep you guys on or not.

AL: Holy shit.

JERRY: I mean, it's something I'll have to think over. (*He turns and starts out*)

LOU: Jesus!

AL (*Running after JERRY*): Jerry, for God sakes, I brought you in on this!

JERRY stops and looks at AL.

JERRY: And, in the final reckoning, I will certainly take that into account. (*He exits regally*)

AL: That motherfucker! Unbelievable! *After all I've done for him!*

LOU: You told me that you *knew* this guy.

AL: Lou, Lou, I knew him like *myself*!

LOU: Well, then this makes sense.

AL: Oh great, this is just what I need.

JERRY returns with a look of amazement.

JERRY: Al . . . ?

AL (*To* LOU, *sotto voce, apprehensive*): Now what?

LOU *shrugs, as worried as* AL.

JERRY: Al, I think I've just had a major emotional breakthrough.
Al, just before I left, there was a look in your eyes. Yours
and Lou's . . . Al, no one has ever looked at me like that.
Never. *Never.* You know what it was? (*Pause*) It was *fear.*
(*It's as if* JERRY *has not realized the implications of this word
"fear" till just now*) . . . Al, you were *afraid* of me! I've
never felt anything so fantastic in my entire life! (*A wild,
delicious smile spreads across* JERRY's *face*) FUCK YOU! (AL
stares back, startled. JERRY *starts to advance on* AL *with a
menacing gleam in his eyes*) Fuck you . . . ! (AL *backs away,
scared.* JERRY *keeps moving in*) Fuck you, fuck you! Fuck
you! Fuck you. Fuck you, fuck-you-fuck-you fuck *you!* You
fuck! (JERRY, *seeing* AL *cowering in fear, turns to* LOU,
thrilled) Lou! "The Fuck-You Power!" It's unbefuckinliev-
able! (*He turns back to* AL) Don't worry about me. No more.
I'm with you. (*Taking in* LOU) With the *both* of you. (*To
them both*) We shared blood, we shared shit, we share THIS!
We're in this fuckin' muthafuckin' thing *together!* I am saying
yes to this fuckin' deal. For us all! *It's a fuckin' GO!*

Exit JERRY, *with a newfound strength. It takes* AL *and* LOU *a
moment to recover. Pause.*

AL (*Finally*): . . . Wha'dya think?

LOU: He'll never take the terms.

AL: Of course he will.

LOU (*Shaking her head no*): He's flying much too high. He's
gonna break, he's gonna snap, he's gonna crash.

AL: Lou, the man's been *hooked*!

LOU: And he can come *unhooked*, like *that*!

AL: No more. Not now. Lou, he's come too far. If he does not grab this, he has one place left to go—*under*, and straight down into oblivion. Even sharks will not notice him as he sinks. The sum of his life will be zero. At most, there may be a rumor that he lived. No no, I'll give odds. He's been *hooked*. (*JERRY returns, dazed*) Mind you, I'm not saying he won't resist.

LOU (*Staring at JERRY*): "*Resist*"?

AL turns and looks at JERRY. JERRY stares out, numb.

AL (*As calmly as possible*): . . . So, how'd it go?

JERRY (*In shock*): Not too well . . . This is not going to work out, Al. Just take my word for it, all right? I mean, it's more than a hunch. Come on.

AL: Jerry . . . !

JERRY: I'll explain in the car! Now come ON!

NIRVANA enters as JERRY tries to lead AL out.

AL: JERRY—!

JERRY sees NIRVANA and stops.

NIRVANA: Look, I meant it. You don't have to take this deal. Really, no one's making you.

JERRY: I'll bear that in mind. (*To* AL *and* LOU, *sotto voce*) She's crazier than we thought, Al. By a *lot*. *More* than a lot. Now come ON!

AL: Jerry—!

JERRY: *She wants my balls.*

AL: . . . *What!?*

JERRY: Sssh! She wants my balls.

AL: Your *balls?*

JERRY: My balls! Yes! My fuckin' BALLS! Those are her TERMS! She's got a knife and a fuckin' *sterilizer!*

AL: She *showed* you this?

JERRY: She said they're in a room nearby. Said it's like a small operating room. With a doctor in residence. Shit, man! I mean like holy fuckin' shit!

AL: Jerry. Calm down.

JERRY: Calm *down?* She's got a surgeon waiting to cut off my balls, you want me to calm *DOWN?*

AL: Jerry—

NIRVANA: I'd do it myself, but I don't really feel competent.

JERRY: From lunchtime on, this day has just gotten worse and worse.

AL: Jerry, no one's going to make you do anything you don't want. Okay? Maybe I can renegotiate.

JERRY: It's not worth it.

AL (*Appalled*): Not *worth* it!? Are you fuckin' *crazy*?

JERRY: Al—!

AL: Let me handle it! CALM DOWN! (*Turning to* NIRVANA) We came here in good faith. And if you are not going to negotiate in good faith, I don't care, fuck this film, goodbye, because my partners and I do not work like this, all right? That's the truth, that's the fuckin' truth. There it is. Take it or leave it.

NIRVANA: I thought my terms were fair.

AL: Hey, to *you* they're fair, you don't have testicles. Now, do we talk or not? If not, we're gone. We're history.

NIRVANA *signals him to approach.*

LOU (*Sotto voce*): Good luck.

AL: Thanks. (*He heads over to* NIRVANA)

LOU (*To* JERRY): You did right to turn it down.

JERRY: *I* thought so.

NIRVANA *and* AL *confer at the side in heated whispers.*

LOU: *Another* film'll come along.

JERRY (*Eyes on* NIRVANA *and* AL—*nervous*): Sure.

Pause.

LOU: Maybe not as good as *this* . . .

The idea of that strikes JERRY *like a stab wound.*

JERRY: . . . It's not like I'm a spoilsport!

LOU: I know that. We know that. (*AL returns*) How'd it go?

AL: Good. Very good. Very very good. (*To* JERRY) Jerry, this
woman likes you a *lot*. I mean, like, you made a very strong
impression. She has faith in you. She wants this thing to
work. All right?

LOU: So?

AL: I knocked it down to one.

JERRY: . . . *One?*

AL: The choice of which—left or right—is yours.

LOU: Wow!

AL: I know. I'm kind of amazed at this myself!

JERRY: Are you fuckin' *mad?*

AL: Jerry, I swear, for a deal like this, a one-ball give-back isn't
bad.

JERRY: This isn't happening. This can't be happening.

AL: Jerry, she is giving you a fucking ball!

JERRY: I don't *need* a fuckin' ball, I've got TWO!

LOU: I thought she's taking one.

JERRY: She isn't taking ANY!

AL: Jerry, Jerry—

JERRY: You want me to give up a fuckin' *ball* for a fucking *DEAL*?

AL: I want you to *CONSIDER* giving up a ball for a deal.

JERRY: Fuck you.

AL: Jerry, what she is asking you to do is symbolic.

JERRY: Here we go again!

AL: But do you know what it's symbolic *of*?

JERRY: Al—!

AL: It's symbolic of *sacrifice*!

JERRY: What symbolic? It *IS* sacrifice!

AL: It's a very powerful symbol. I understand your reticence.

JERRY: Good. Give her one of yours.

AL: I would if I could but I can't.

JERRY: . . . Huh?

LOU: He has none left to give.

JERRY: *What!?*

AL: It took one ball to get the option on this thing.

JERRY: You're shitting me.

AL (*To NIRVANA*): Tell 'm.

NIRVANA shrugs.

JERRY: Oh my God.

AL: My other ball I gave up years ago in a deal that sounded kinda good at the time.

JERRY: Al!

AL: So don't talk to me about losing balls! One fuckin' ball, that's all she wants! I mean, what's the big fuckin' deal? (*Sotto voce*) She's got a screw loose, right? What else is new? (*Back to normal voice*) You want the deal, you take the terms! It's her *life* that's on the line! She needs to know she can count on us. Is that wrong? I don't know. To me it was worth a ball. I only had one left—I gave it up. I would not have given two. You, you motherfucker, you've *got* two!

JERRY: Al—

AL: The fuckin' world, I just don't understand. I mean, like, what do you value? Is she asking for your cock?

JERRY: Al . . .

AL: You'll still get it up. I still get it up. Lou?

LOU: What?

AL: Do I get it up?

LOU: Sometimes.

AL: There you are. It works, the plumbing works. I mean, really, man, I just don't understand what the fuck is wrong.

JERRY starts to laugh.

JERRY: This day is actually getting *worse!* (*His laughter approaches hysteria*)

AL: I'm sorry, Jerry. I can see you're upset. You've gone through a lot today.

JERRY stops laughing. A sudden, terrible thought has just occurred.

JERRY (*Staring at AL in horror*): That's why you brought me in on this.

AL: Jer—

JERRY (*Stunned*): You *knew* this was coming . . .

AL: Jerry, listen—

JERRY: That's why you needed someone who had balls!

AL: Jer—

JERRY: Eating shit was an hors d'oeuvre to this!

AL: Jerry—

JERRY (*Fury rising*): Wasn't it? . . . *Wasn't it?* (*He looks AL right in the eyes. But AL says nothing. His silence is all the answer JERRY needs*) . . . I can't fuckin' believe it. *You knew this was coming!*

AL (*Trying to make light of it*): Jerry—

JERRY: Boy, you are a FUCK!

NIRVANA (*To AL*): Let him go.

AL: *No!*

NIRVANA: I don't want to do this film anymore.

AL: NO NO! PLEASE! DON'T SAY THAT! IT'S A GREAT
FILM! I KNOW IT IS! LIKE *GONE WITH THE WIND!*
ONLY BIGGER, BETTER! I CAN SENSE THESE
THINGS! SO CAN LOU! PLEASE! HOLD ON! Jerry, have
I ever told you my view of life?

JERRY: No, Al. But I'd like to hear.

AL: I see life essentially, *essentially*, as a mystery. Which is to
say, though there is undoubtedly much more to it than that,
essentially . . . that is what I see. (*Pause*) I move through
life like a shadow. Footsteps in the dark, that is what I am.
A passing figment of imagination! "The weed of crime bears
bitter fruit"—Lamont Cranston. Jerry, sometimes I lay
awake at night and I think, I am without substance. And yet
I exist! *How is this possible?* You catchin' what I'm sayin'
here?

JERRY (*His own terror suddenly showing through*): No.

AL: I am saying, here is an opportunity for all of us to have
substance.

JERRY: . . . Money.

AL: More.

JERRY: A lot of money.

AL: Money is a *sign*.

JERRY: Money is symbolic.

AL: There ya go!

JERRY: Symbolic of substance.

AL: Money *tells* you you have substance.

JERRY: Without money . . .

AL: Nothing but a shadow. (*Moving JERRY out of NIRVANA's earshot*) Which is what we are right now. *We don't have to be!* We can be major players, Jerry. Major players in the Big Picture. The Sands of Time, Jerry—that's what this is all about. And you're worried about a fuckin' testicle?

JERRY (*Scared*): Oh God . . . !

NIRVANA: Jerry. You don't have to do this if you don't want.

JERRY (*Barely audible*): I know.

NIRVANA: If you don't, it will simply mean *that* was the sign I needed. And I'll know this film wasn't meant to be. (*JERRY struggles with his fear*) I'm sorry, Jerry, but I can't let you in for less. If I did, how would I know I could count on you in the crunch? How would I know that you love me? (*Pause*) In my position, I'm sure you would do the same . . . We all have to prove ourselves *sometime*.

Long pause. JERRY struggles. He wants to do it, he does! You can see it in his face . . . But he just can't. NIRVANA, seeing his reticence, turns away with a sigh of disappointment. LOU, seeing NIRVANA's disenchantment, jumps in.

LOU (*To AL*): Get him out o' here.

AL: . . . What?

LOU: He's had his chance. Go on, get him out. Get rid of him.

JERRY: *What!?*

LOU: Shut up! I'm fuckin' sick of you! You're a fuckin' disaster! (*To NIRVANA*) We'll get you someone else.

JERRY: No! Wait!

LOU: Hey! You had your chance. (*To NIRVANA*) Honey. I'm sorry, very sorry.

JERRY: *Wait!*

LOU: You *had* your fuckin' chance! Now get the fuck out! (*To NIRVANA*) You can't work with shit like this! Shit like this will bring the project down. I'd rather not *do* this film than work with shit like this! No money in the *world* is worth that! You couldn't PAY me enough for that!

JERRY: *FUCK YOU!* (*Everyone turns and stares at him*) Who the fuck are you to talk to me like that? What the fuck do *you* know about what I've been through? And I don't mean just today either, I mean in my life, my LIFE! All right? Okay? So *FUCK OFF!* I mean, what the fuck are *you* giving up for this, a tit? I don't see you giving up SHIT for this! This is not an easy thing this woman's asking me to do, not easy, not at all; by no *STRETCH OF THE IMAGINATION* is this an easy thing to do! Or do you think it is? . . . I mean, you think I'm just gonna say, "Here, honey. Sure, please, feel free, take 'em! And while you're at it, take anything else you want—take my fingers, take my ears." FUCK YOU! *You* get out of here! *YOUUUUUU* get out o' here! 'Cause I'm not moving. (*Pointing to NIRVANA*) If she wants me out, I will go. Not you, not Al, *she* . . . gives the word to me around this place, not you. (*Turning to NIRVANA*) I'm in.

LOU: Bullshit.

JERRY: Yeah? Fuck you, bullshit! You're the one who's bullshit! You and Al. I'm the one she needs. You understand me? *Needs*. We have a connection you will never have. *Never!* (*Turning to* NIRVANA—*strong, resolute*) You want two? Say the word and I will give you two. I will. I mean, if that is what you want, really truly want, two it is, two it fuckin' is! Which is not to say I wouldn't much prefer giving none. I would. I mean, hey, you think I'm crazy? Of COURSE I would! Or, in a pinch, just one. Of course I would. *But!* Here's the point: if two is what it takes to make you know that I'm with you, come what may, for better or for worse, two it is, two it fuckin' is. And I will leave this decision entirely to you. You say you need to know you can trust in me? Well, I will trust in you. In your judgment and your goodness. 'Cause you know what?—the gods did not send me to you. They sent you to me! This film is going to set clocks ticking in a whole new fuckin' direction. This film is going to make fuckin' HISTORY! And I am going to be part of it! (*To* LOU *and* AL, *with controlled ferocity*) And no one's going to fuckin' stop me. NO ONE! "*MOBY-FUCKIN'-DICK!*" Melville *knew* where his book would lead, he fuckin' KNEW! (*Stunned—a sudden revelation*) That's why he wrote the book! (*To* NIRVANA, *with steely calm, confident as hell*) Where's the operating room?

NIRVANA: In there. Just past the steam room.

NIRVANA *gestures. A door slides open—a door previously unnoticed. Steam emerges. We can see white tile.* JERRY *stares into the steam. The sight takes his breath away. He takes a deep breath and marches in, bravely, heroically,* NIRVANA *by his side. The door shuts.* AL *and* LOU *stare at each other, stunned.*

LOU: . . . He *did* it!

AL: I can't fuckin' believe it!

LOU: I thought you were sure.

AL: I *was*, but *still* . . . (*He looks around in awe. Then so does she. The idea that it's really happened, and what that means for them, is only beginning to dawn. Finally—almost spooked*) . . . Lou, this is not an accident.

LOU: What?

AL: This, all this, what's happened here. *This is not an accident.*

LOU (*Softly—in awe*): . . . I know. (*A scream can be heard from the steam room. It's* JERRY. AL *and* LOU *wince—*LOU *in sympathy,* AL *with empathy. It takes a moment for them to regain composure. Deeply moved*) . . . Good man.

AL: Yeah, good fuckin' man.

LOU: Not many men have a friend like that.

AL: And to think: once upon a time I did him *dirt!*

LOU: You were different then.

AL: I was like some monster then.

LOU: Good thing you changed.

AL: If I hadn't, this would not have worked.

LOU: I know.

AL (*Reverent gesture upward*): *He* saw.

LOU: Of course He saw. He sees everything.

AL: . . . And He smiled on us.

The lights begin to change ever so slightly. LOU shivers a bit. A startled look comes over her face.

LOU: Al . . . (*She seems spooked*) . . . I have a feeling . . . (*Sotto voce*) . . . I think He's smiling down on us right now.

AL (*Sotto voce*): I can feel it, too!

LOU: It's like . . .

AL (*A bit spooked himself*): Yeah. I know. *Very weird.*

LOU: Indescribable.

Pause. They seem almost scared.

AL: Wonder why He smiles on some . . . but not on others.

LOU: I don't know. It's like, you know . . . a mystery.

AL nods. They stare out at the pool and the sky in an awe bordering on terror. LOU snuggles up next to him, as if chilled. Same for him.
   Slow fade to black.

Curtain